"JESS, DON'T YOU SEE, FROME WILL KILL YOU . . .

Jess, don't do it this way! Frome's got to pay for what he's done. But we'll go to Miles City. We'll go to the Stockgrower's Association and make a charge." Elizabeth tried to restrain him.

"No!" he said.

He got through the door. He heard her call, but he pulled the door shut behind him. For a moment he stood in the darkness; he was no longer shaking; his anger was a terrible, cold calmness. He peered, looking for his horse. He took a step, and something stiffened the hairs at the back of his neck. Not ten feet away was the motionless shape of a man . . .

Loudon made a try for his gun. He saw the red smear of flame and heard the crash of another gun. Or was the roar in his own head? He reached out blindly. He grasped at air, and grasping, fell . . .

Books by Norman A. Fox

The Badlands Beyond
The Rawhide Years
The Thirsty Land

Published by POCKET BOOKS

NORMAN A. FOX

The Badlands Beyond

POCKET BOOKS
New York London Toronto Sydney Tokyo

This book is a work of fiction. Names, characters, places and incidents are either the product of the author's imagination or are used fictitiously. Any resemblance to actual events or locales or persons, living or dead, is entirely coincidental.

POCKET BOOKS, a division of Simon & Schuster Inc.
1230 Avenue of the Americas, New York, NY 10020

Published by arrangement with Dodd, Mead & Co.
Library of Congress Catalog Card Number: 57-7133

ISBN: 0-671-64820-9

First Pocket Books printing July 1989

10 9 8 7 6 5 4 3 2 1

Printed in the U.S.A.

For BUTCH BYERSDORF, upon whose knowledge of the Old West I have leaned again and again

Contents

The Badlands Beyond

1

River Town

FROM LONG NINE RANCH NORTHWARD TO CRAGGY POINT settlement on the Missouri, the range lay so big and open and empty that Jess Loudon felt he was standing still, even when he used the whip and got the square-top buggy clattering harder. Around him the land spread, thinly carpeted by bunch grass curing in the stand, the hills lying low on the horizon, and over all a gray pall of smoke where forest fires burned in western Montana, half the Territory away. Loudon wished the journey done. Today this country turned his mind to thoughts better left alone.

He'd been hours on the road. He'd left Long Nine at dawn after hitching up a spring wagon only to have to put it and the team away and get out this buggy instead. The change had been Ollie Scoggins' idea. Scoggins ramrodded Long Nine for Peter Frome and had a right to ideas. The foreman had said, "She won't be toting luggage a buggy won't haul." Scoggins had muttered something about hurrying. Trouble was, a man got only an edge of Ollie Scoggins' thinking these days. Loudon guessed Ollie was tussling with something too big for him; plenty of times he'd caught the foreman gazing out to the rim of the badlands. Scoggins had thrust a Winchester into the buggy this morning.

Frome hadn't even showed, Loudon recalled. Come to think about it, he hadn't set eyes on Frome for a couple of days.

Now it was nearly noon, though the sun was hard to find, lost up there in the smoke pall. Loudon tried turning his mind from the dark mood that was made from small frettings about Frome and Scoggins and the trouble shaping up. He wished himself with Long Nine's crew catching up with late-born calves and building a sage and buffalo-chip branding fire in some coulee. Today's chore was a hell of a one for a cowboy, a job Frome should be doing himself. He gave the horse an extra flick of the whip.

Within an hour he was going down grade, the land falling away before him and the river stretching below. Bluffs and the broken rim of the badlands limited his view, but Loudon looked hard for a steamboat's smoke. A few willows showed, none too green this dry summer, and sprawled among these was Craggy Point. Toward the settlement he wheeled, coming at last into the single street and pulling to a stop before the livery.

Ike Nicobar appeared in the gloom of the doorway. His leathery face brightened. "So it's you, Jess."

Loudon climbed down. "Give this broomtail the best you got, Ike," he said and shook hands with the old man. Ike was so whiskered that he might have been hiding in ambush. Rheumatism had bent him down; and Loudon felt sad, seeing him and remembering how Ike had once swung a buffalo gun as though it were a willow twig.

"An Idaho hoss," Ike said, looking at the Long Nine animal. "A damn' paint, bought from the Nez Perces, I'll bet. Frome thinks more of money than he does of good horses." He peered in the buggy and saw the rifle; his face clouded. "What's Frome going to do, Jess?"

"About the trouble?" Loudon shrugged. "Better ask what Singleton's going to do. Or Cottrell, or Lathrop's Looped L, or any of the other cow outfits. Every ranch from here to Miles has got a stake in this thing."

"They'll do whatever Frome does," Nicobar said, dead certain.

Loudon said, "Don't let it fret you, Ike."

Nicobar's seamed face puckered. "There's a passel of boys scattered around, Jess. Some as hunted the buffler, like us. Some as cut wood for the steamboats. Wolfers and trappers. Pilgrims who come to mine in the Judiths. What's them to do that's left over from the old days? Take a riding job like your'n, or a hostler's job like mine? Some don't shine to takin' orders from a boss."

Loudon said, "The man who's tied to a boss won't be drifting into trouble."

"The way Joe McSween's drifting?" Nicobar shook his head. "Maybe so. But it's the stockmen and the railroads that's ruint the country. First they built the Northern Pacific through. Now Jim Hill's coming in with another. Damn it, Jess, what was wrong with steamboats to do the fetchin' and carryin'?"

Loudon looked toward the landing. "I'm meeting the *Prairie Belle.*"

"The *Belle*'ll make it this afternoon. Some of the boys sighted her at the mouth of Redwater this morning."

Loudon nodded. "Frome's niece is coming in. I'm

here to tote her to Long Nine. Twenty men in the bunkhouse, and I had to get picked for the chore." He looked around. "Anybody in town?"

"Joe McSween," Nicobar said. "You wouldn't be interested in who else. Maybe you don't even want any truck with Joe, now that he's riding with the badlanders." He climbed into the buggy to wheel it around to the wagon yard, moving slow and carefully, his aches so plain as to give Loudon a twist inside. Nicobar's face showed a sudden bright curiosity. "Didn't ye winter at Clem Latcher's hay ranch last year, Jess?"

"Sure, Ike. I rode the river and chopped water holes in the ice. Frome's learned that you got to keep cattle from going out and falling in air holes. Latcher's place was warm and handy to the job." He said this straight faced, wanting to grin at the way Nicobar was flanking the real question. "Why did you ask about Latcher's?"

Nicobar said craftily, "That Addie Latcher. Ye must 'a' got to know her right well."

Loudon grinned. "Clem was always around."

"What kind of a woman be she, Jess?"

"The kind to put on her best Sunday-go-to-meeting dress and a hat covered with fooforaw to sit around a log shack on a winter evening."

"To please Clem? Or to please you?"

"To please herself," Loudon said.

Nicobar unwrapped the reins from around the whipstock, his face puckering again. "What became of the buffler, Jess?" His mind was like a bird on a bush, hopping here and there. "One day the prairie was black with 'em. Now there's nothing but bones to show. Where did the buffler go?"

"We killed 'em, Ike," Loudon said gently. He reached under the buggy seat and brought out a shirt-wrapped package. From it he hauled out a pint of whiskey which he handed to Nicobar. "Fetched this for you from Miles City, Ike. It'll roll down smoother than the stuff they make hereabouts to slip across the river to the Indians."

"Thank ye, Jess," Nicobar said, thrusting the bottle inside his buckskin jumper. "Thank ye right kindly."

The buggy went swinging around a corner of the building, and Jess Loudon stood hipshot while he shaped a cigarette. About him Craggy Point squatted, a few business establishments, several saloons, a steamboat landing. The summer heat was softened here by a river breeze which stirred the willows. An ugly town of ugly pleasures, Loudon decided, and looked toward the badlands beyond, whence the stealthy ones came. Ike's talk had reminded him of the shaping trouble again—"What's Frome going to do, Jess?"—but damned if he'd let it worry him. He was his own man, and he had made his choice.

He stood sleepy lidded, drawing in every sight and sound and smell of the town. All his twenty-odd years he had followed ways that made for a sharp eye. Cow camp and buffalo trail had shaped him, giving him a limber way of walking and a limber way of living. Too limber to shut out an old pardner like Joe McSween, he supposed. When he fired his smoke, he watched, over the match, the lone horse hitched in front of the Assiniboine Saloon. Joe always favored good Texas geldings, although the sloppy way he sat a saddle belied his ability to pick the good from the bad. "You'll end up with a broken neck," Loudon had told him more than once.

Still Loudon stood by the livery, wanting to make talk with McSween yet not wanting to. He looked toward the river, hoping for a sight of the steamboat.

Over yonder stretched fine grass country, but that land was mostly Indian reservation. No Frome there to spill Long Nine cattle far and wide.

Loudon shrugged, dropped his cigarette and set his boot upon it, then turned toward the Assiniboine.

He came into the crude, dusty saloon to find only Joe McSween and the bartender. McSween had his elbows on the bar and was mildly drunk. "Howdy, Jess," he said with a grin and reached for the bottle before him. He was young and careless; and looking at him, Loudon thought how that grin could melt a man down to the softness of axle grease. He'd never been any hand at wrangling the serious things with Joe.

"I've been hoping for a chance to talk with you, Joe," he said. At the rear of the barroom was a door giving into a cubbyhole equipped with table and chairs and a bunk for a man to sleep off his pleasuring. He jerked his head. "In there."

"No," McSween said with alcoholic sharpness. "Not in there."

"Why not?"

"I do a chore for Idaho Jack Ives now and then. You know that, Jess. I wouldn't want you to go in there, and neither would he."

Loudon said, "The hell with Ives," and crossed over and swung the door inward. He heard the quick rustle of footsteps inside and knew that his voice had carried through the planking and given warning. The cubbyhole was empty to his eye. His mind was flung back to his asking Ike Nicobar who was in town and Ike's saying, "Joe McSween. You wouldn't be interested in who else." He closed the door.

McSween asked hotly, "Why did you have to do that?"

"To see what Ives was keeping hid."

McSween said, "Look, Jess. Ives should be here by now. You'd better clear out."

Loudon came to the bar and nodded at the barkeep, who placed a glass before him. Loudon tilted McSween's bottle and filled his own glass and McSween's and said, "I'm buying," and planked money on the bar. He winked at McSween, and that took the tightness out of Joe.

"Plenty of trail herds coming up to Miles, Joe," Loudon said. "The bedding grounds across the Yellowstone are crawling with them. Long Nine's got one coming in later in the season. Why don't you sign up with one of those drovers and go back to Texas or Kansas for more beef?"

"A hard life and a dull one, Jess. Like working for Frome. What's that getting you besides saddle sores?"

"Frome's a big man, Joe, and he's getting bigger. I figure that the man who works for him will grow with him. I don't aim to end up like Ike Nicobar."

"Or like me, eh? Got your eye on the foremanship, Jess?"

"Bigger than that, Joe. A spread of my own someday, maybe."

"So meantime you'll walk in Frome's shadow and that way you'll get as big as Frome. You always was ambitious, Jess. By the way, what's Frome going to do about the rustling?"

"What do you think?"

McSween laughed. "Stir up a lot of dust."

"Joe," Loudon said, "I wouldn't want to see any of that dust get into *your* eyes. I came in here to tell you to pull out. Will you take that advice?"

"I'd rather take another drink," McSween said and downed the one he held.

"I'm telling you because we worked together for

three seasons—you and me and Ike Nicobar—until the time came to stack the heavy guns and drift. Hell, man, I wouldn't want to be riding with the outfit that'll be closing in on your crew some dark night."

"Idaho Jack takes care of us, Jess. He's smart. Smarter than Frome thinks."

Loudon nodded again toward the cubbyhole, feeling his belly jump the way it did when a piece of tainted meat hit it. "Smart enough to send you in ahead to line up a deal like that for him, eh? Joe, I know Jack Ives. He was one of those gamblers who came into the Judith during the mining boom that went bust. Since then he's been doing his sleeping when the sun's up. He'll play you like a card from the bottom of the deck. And when he's finished using you, he'll throw you into the discard."

McSween colored. "Hell, Jess, I don't need my nose blowed." He looked toward that rear room. "How Jack takes his fun is his own affair."

"Not when he uses you to guard the door."

"I'll string along till he's proved himself less than a man at a man's game."

Loudon got the feeling he was battering against stone. "And maybe that will be too late." He lifted his head, his attention caught by a flurry of sound out on the street. "Riders," he announced. "About a dozen, I'd guess. Coming in from the east, from the rough country."

"Ives," McSween said and looked soberer. "You'd better drift, Jess."

"Not unless you come with me, Joe—to start south for Miles and a job."

McSween said harshly, "Dammit, you heard me on that!"

Through the dirt-glazed window Loudon saw milling horses stir up dust as Ives and his men drew into a knot and dismounted before the hitchrack. They came in with no talk, Ives leading them. When he saw Loudon, he moved along the wall instead of toward the bar and made a flat, quick gesture with his hands that spread his men out. Loudon recognized some who had been buffalo hunters. None paid him a howdy. He had, he reflected, built a fence when he'd put his name down on Frome's payroll. Then another thought struck him. Queer, considering that cubby-hole, that Ives had brought his pack with him. Had the man got so he never rode alone?

Joe McSween said, "Drink, Jack?" making it unnecessarily loud.

Ives, Loudon noticed, still wore gambler's black, though he had changed professions. He was a tall man, pinch waisted and smooth shaven, the kind to ride along admiring his shadow, but there was something of the cat in him. It showed most in his smile.

"So it's one of Long Nine's boys," he said. "That's good. Now we'll know what Mr. Frome is planning to do. Eh, friend?"

Loudon had put his back to the bar. So had McSween. Loudon said, "Frome hasn't told me. But I can guess." He remembered the Winchester Scoggins had put in the buggy; a hand gun would be better in quarters as close as these. "And my guess is that Frome's going to hang every rustler between here and the Yellowstone."

Ives stiffened. "And will you be riding with Frome when that chore is pulled off?"

The beating thought in Loudon was that there still was time to hunt a rat hole, but McSween was beside him and that made the difference. He had to prove something to McSween. "I reckon," he said.

Ives looked about at his men. "You heard him." His men moved ever so slightly, putting themselves farther apart.

Then McSween said tautly, "Friend of mine, Jack."

Ives looked hard at McSween. "You sure about that, Joe?"

"Certain sure."

"Friend of yours, too, maybe," Loudon said, making it careless. "Next time you get her hid out in a room waiting for you, Ives, give her warning. Tell her that when she ducks behind the door, she'd better not leave her hat on the table. Especially a fooforaw hat a man would remember!"

Loudon heard Joe McSween suck in a hard, rasping breath.

The dark blood of anger rose in Ives' face. "Damn you, you're needling me!"

"Then," Loudon said, "that makes it personal and just between the two of us." This was like poker! A man took the cards that came to his hand, and if they weren't good enough, he had nothing left but bluff.

But Ives shook his head. "No, friend. We're not twisting this around to suit *your* fancy." He looked straight at Loudon, but he spoke to his men. "Easy pickings, boys. And one less against us when Long Nine starts its clean-up."

Loudon said pointedly to McSween, "A man playing a man's game, Joe?"

McSween drew his gun. "I sent for him when he hit town, Jack. Do you understand? I had business with him." With his free hand he reached into his pocket and brought out five silver dollars and stacked them on the bar. All the while he kept his eyes on Idaho Jack. "I've owed you that five for two seasons, Jess," McSween said. "Take it and get out."

Loudon said, "I stomp my own snakes, Joe. You know that."

"Take it!" McSween insisted.

Loudon pocketed the money. "You coming along with me, Joe?"

McSween said, "You proved your point, you loco damn' fool. I'm beholden for the drink and the lesson. Now will you get the hell out!"

Loudon said, "You need any gear for a long ride, you come to me."

He heard the steamboat whistle then, shrill and clear on the river. "Time for a working man to be getting along," he said. Ives stood there, sour and troubled, held by McSween's gun, held by uncertainty. Loudon, still with one last worry, asked McSween, "You going to be all right?"

"Sure," McSween said, and his face showed bitterness. "I'm too high a card to be tossed into the discard. A smart gambler wouldn't throw away his ace."

"True," Loudon said and crossed toward the door, his boots beating out a hard sound that broke the holding silence.

2

Steamboat At The Landing

HE STRODE THE BOARDWALK TRYING NOT TO THINK HOW close he'd come to big trouble in the Assiniboine. He still had that nagging worry concerning Joe McSween, and just beyond the saloon he paused for a moment, waiting. Let a gun sound and he would be back in there, his own gun out. His shoulders hunched as he canted his head, listening. Nothing. Ives would be walking soft and talking soft around Joe McSween from here on out, Loudon judged. He walked on then, and soon he began to laugh. He'd hoped to show up Ives as the kind who needed a crew to do his fighting, and so show McSween the light. A good day's work!

Yonder on the river, the *Prairie Belle,* glimpsed through the willows, loomed big, Pittsburg made and cut down for the Missouri River trade. Loudon judged that her cabins would accommodate no more than thirty passengers. Cargo would be annuity goods for the Indians and merchandise for the stores of Fort Benton and maybe mining machinery to be toted overland to the Last Chance diggings. That old stern wheel was a-sloshing, and Loudon got the feeling to be gone that a man got when he heard a locomotive's whistle in the night.

He'd ridden these packets more than once. He remembered coming up from St. Louis with Ike Nicobar and Joe McSween after a spree that had cost them all of a season's buffalo kill, and he knew what such a journey gave a man in the way of memories. A month out of St. Louis, the *Prairie Belle* would have breasted the June rise, while Miss Elizabeth Bower, lately of Ohio, had probably scampered around the decks, exclaiming over each new turn of the river. Maybe they'd glimpsed buffalo; maybe they'd even been held up by some last remnant of the northern herds crossing the river. There'd have been bright moonlit nights and heady sunlit days and the birds singing and the smell of thousands of flowers coming off the prairie.

Craggy Point would shortly be turning out for the docking, though it wasn't likely there'd be much unloaded here in the way of either cargo or passengers. Frome's niece, of course. A barrel of whiskey for a saloon, maybe. A bolt of calico. Loudon got to the landing and found it nearly deserted.

A lone man, looking aimless and forlorn, sat on the edge of the wharf, his legs dangling. He looked up at Loudon sullenly. "Hello, Jess."

"Howdy, Clem," Loudon said and was suddenly embarrassed.

A colorless man, Clem Latcher, with a sandy, bleached mustache and a soft face and eyes like a licked dog's. He was from the East, and rumor said he had education and money. He nodded toward the oncoming packet. "Got somebody aboard?"

"Frome's niece," Loudon said.

Latcher nodded. "I remember her. She was out here

two years ago and stayed the summer. About eighteen then. A nice girl." He drew his long legs up and wrapped his arms around them. "What's Frome going to do about the rustling, Jess?"

Loudon said, "You'll know when the time comes. You'll be in on it. With you selling hay to Long Nine, you're practically part of the ranch. That gives you a stake in the clean-up."

Latcher shrugged slightly. "I don't care," he said in a dead voice. "But Frome shouldn't be letting his niece come at a time like this. I can guess what he'll do. He'll go in for wholesale hangings. Jess, has one man the right to set himself up in judgment over others?"

"Where's the law to do it for him?"

"Frome's a good man, I think," Latcher said. "But here he's about to take on the powers of judge, jury, and executioner. What will that do to him? I wonder if Frome's thought about that." He looked away from Loudon. "Addie's in town. Seen her?"

"No," Loudon said flatly.

"She took off this morning, dressed in her best. I trailed her here; but after all, I can't knock on every door in Craggy Point. I thought she might be waiting to catch the boat on to Benton. She has a dull life at our place. You saw that last winter, Jess."

Loudon fumbled out his tobacco and papers and made his hands busy, not liking the turn Latcher's talk had taken. No sense in a man's showing his hurts and sniveling over them. He offered the makings, and as Latcher leaned closer to reach them, he smelled the whiskey on Latcher. For a moment Latcher's eyes met his, and Loudon saw the torment there and knew it had been no sociable drinking that had given Latcher his breath. He and Latcher had spent many an evening at the checker-board last winter, while Addie had sat watching, making her sultry presence felt.

"She probably came in to buy some dress goods," Loudon said. "A woman works off steam that way, same as a man does spreeing."

"Joe McSween," Latcher said. "He's in town, too."

"Yes."

"You must know Joe pretty well."

Loudon lit his cigarette and offered the match to Latcher. "Hell, Clem, Joe wouldn't come within lariat length of another man's wife."

"Ives rode in too, with his whole pack."

"A pretty good sign that he didn't come to meet a woman. Use your head, Clem."

"I'll find the man," Latcher said. "I'll find him, and I'll kill him!"

"And what will that change?" Loudon asked.

Latcher angrily flung his cigarette into the river. "Do you think it's easy to live with it or talk about it? Here I am hedging around with you, trying to get answers to questions I don't dare come right out and ask. Confound it, Jess, I've gone through a lot of hell!"

"Take her some place else, Clem. A million miles away from here."

Latcher shook his head. "We've been married ten years now. There have been plenty of other places. The scenery's changed, but she hasn't."

"Then it's you that's got to change," Loudon said. "An exciting woman needs an exciting man."

"You don't understand, Jess. It's a disease with her—a disease you'll find in the histories, if you read between the lines. Jezebel, Delilah, Cleopatra . . . they were all sick with her sickness."

"Oh, hell!" Loudon said.

The packet was swinging in now. Queer, Loudon

thought, how it could kick up so much white water out of that muddy river. The white water was there all the time, running deep, just as you could get talk out of Latcher about killing a man, while on the surface Latcher looked rabbity.

Craggy Point's people were drifting toward the landing, saloonmen and gamblers and merchants and outlanders. Loudon glimpsed the whiskered face of Ike Nicobar. Ives wasn't in sight, though most of his men were in the gathering crowd. Joe McSween came along the street, astride his Texas gelding. McSween had no interest in the packet. He swung his horse southward and took the wagon road that crawled up the slope to the flat country beyond the breaks. Loudon cupped his hands to his mouth and shouted, "Hey, Joe!"

McSween swung around in his saddle and gave Loudon a wave.

"Come back here and get your five dollars, you crazy fool!"

"Keep it to remember me by," McSween shouted. He jogged his horse to a trot. "I'm heading for the Prickly, and Miles."

The sloshing of the packet's paddle wheel became a close thunder, blotting out all other sound; and when Loudon turned about, he could see the scurrying crew and the faces lined along the rail of the boiler deck. The wheel went dead, the silence so sudden it was like a shout. Deck hands leaped from the low main deck to the wharf and got busy at making the lines fast. Talk buzzed on the landing, people milling about.

Loudon pushed through the crowd and up the lowered plank to the packet and climbed a companionway to the boiler deck. "Miss Bower?" he asked a roustabout, and then he saw her.

She was one of those who'd crowded the rail, but she had turned back toward her cabin door as Loudon came up. He couldn't have told how he knew her. Nothing of Frome in her looks. She was small boned and moved with a quick grace that put him in mind of an antelope. She wore a long-sleeved dress that fitted snugly at the throat. Her face was pretty, and her eyes were placid. Loudon took off his short-brimmed hat and said, "I'm from Long Nine, Miss."

"I don't remember you," she said.

"I'm new. Loudon. Jess Loudon."

"And I'm Elizabeth Bower," she said.

He liked the feel of her handshake. It was good and firm and had no nonsense to it. He said, "You've got luggage, I suppose."

She flung open her cabin door and gestured for him to step inside. She followed him. He saw that the cabin was neat as a pin, and that told him a lot about her. She indicated a small leather-bound trunk in one corner.

"Is that all?" he asked.

She nodded.

"Ollie Scoggins was right," he said.

She smiled, and he saw that she had a kind of roguishness that hadn't at first showed. It gave him the notion that she could kick up her heels if she liked. She said, "I remember Ollie. Tell me, how is he?"

"All right, I guess," Loudon said.

"I supposed my uncle would be here to meet me. Is there anything wrong with him?"

Wrong with Peter Frome? Now what could be wrong with a man who owned more cows than anyone else between the Yellowstone and the Missouri, a man all looked to for leadership, a man who was readying himself to meet outlawry the only way it could be met, head down and head on? Loudon thought now of the talk going around that when Montana became a state, Peter Frome might likely be its first governor—Peter Frome, who kept a library in his ranch-house and talked of schools and churches for the Territory. A man to tie to, Frome.

"No, Miss," he said. "There's nothing wrong with your uncle."

"Are you sure?" she insisted.

Then, suddenly, all the nagging thoughts of that ride up from Long Nine hit at him, and behind that blow was the remembrance of the question every man had put to him in Craggy Point—Ike Nicobar and Joe McSween and Jack Ives and Clem Latcher—that question about what Frome was going to do. And because he damned well knew the answer, he remembered Latcher's fear about her coming; and he said harshly, "I think you'd better not go to the ranch."

This startled her. "And why not?"

"You could stay on this boat till it gets to Benton. It will unload fast and head down river. You could be back in St. Louis in another few weeks. At least you'd have had the trip for your summer's outing."

She looked at him closely. "My uncle told you to suggest such a thing to me?"

He shook his head. "I think he might have, but he's too busy these days even to think about you. We've had rustlers thick as fleas on this range for the last year or so. It's no small thing. The time has come when they've got to be hit—and hit hard. It will be a mighty dirty business. Night riding and hangings. I think you'll find this range too tough for you."

"Do you? And you call that a reason for my not even looking in at Long Nine after coming all this way?"

He frowned. How could he explain something that was only a feeling in his bones? How could he say that it might be better for her never to see Peter Frome at the work that lay ahead? He lifted his hands and let them fall. "I tell you, it will be tough."

She smiled saucily. "I think," she said, "it will be interesting to see how tough it can get."

First he'd had to open Joe McSween's eyes to one thing, and now he had to open this girl's to another. Fury seized him. He reached out and drew her hard against him. He held her tight enough to drive the breath out of her, and he kissed her, making the kiss cruel. He hadn't shaved since yesterday morning, and when he let her go, he saw the red stain on her cheek where he'd rasped her. She stood back from him, too stunned to be angry, her mouth slack, her hair mussed. He said, "You see! You don't know what the hell you're talking about!"

She drew in a sharp breath. He steeled himself for her slap till he saw that she was making a fight with herself. Finally she said, "And that was supposed to make me stay on the boat?"

He shrugged. "It was supposed to show you the difference between where you came from and where you're going."

"I see. I've just been spanked for smiling at your scary story. Is that it?"

He spread his hands. "I've had too much of women for one day."

She said, "Just the same, I'm going to Long Nine."

He shrugged again. "There's a buggy waiting at the livery. I'll bring it around to the landing. We'll eat and get on home." He felt mighty foolish now, like a drunk looking at last night's recklessness. Somewhere in the innards of the packet a signal bell rang; the whistle screamed out over the river and the breaks and the far plains. "You'd better wait for me on the landing," he added. "No need of your walking."

"I don't mind," she said. Then she laughed. "Yours is an inconsistent kind of gallantry, Mr. Loudon."

"Come along," he said and lifted her trunk to his shoulder. She picked up a little blue velvet bonnet from a table and came after him as he stepped to the deck. He heard the quick lisp of her footsteps following his own.

3

Riders By Night

AFTER JESS LOUDON HAD WALKED FROM THE ASSINIBOINE, Idaho Jack Ives held tight to his anger, telling himself there would be another time and place. He could feel Joe McSween's unblinking stare; he was still under McSween's gun. Damn Loudon, standing there sure and cocky, making his speech about Addie Latcher and her hat, turning the situation personal so that the challenge was between one man and another! Well, he might have fooled Loudon and thrown him to the pack if it hadn't been for McSween.

McSween now holstered his gun. He did this carelessly, contemptuously.

Ives smiled. "Do you know, Joe, I don't think you owed him any five dollars."

McSween said, "I'll tell you something, Jack. I don't give a hoot in hell what you think."

About him, Ives could feel his men stiffen. Through the thin walls the sound of the *Prairie Belle*'s paddle came. Ives found something nightmarish in this moment; he knew he should stand up to McSween, but nagging uncertainty still held him back. *Careful now,* he told himself. He judged that he could shade McSween on the draw, but he didn't want the youngster dead. A useful man, McSween.

Take this chore today. Ives had found it risky, he remembered, riding down to Latcher's hay ranch in the sleepy afternoons and taking a chance that Latcher wouldn't come home unexpectedly. Edginess had brought the sweat out and spoiled the fun. Latcher didn't stack very high, but a cuckolded husband could get you from a cutbank and have a rose pinned on him by a jury, if it ever came to that. No, it was much safer having Addie meet him here at the Assiniboine. A handful of silver took care of the bartender, and McSween had packed the note to Addie and stood by at the bar to see that nobody got nosy. McSween could be just as handy in the future.

Ives smiled again. "No call to be jumpy, Joe. I like a man who stands pat for a friend the way you did. Even when that friend rides for Long Nine." He took a step forward. "Belly up, boys. You're all having a drink on me."

Something tight-drawn in his men loosened at once, and they surged toward the bar. Only McSween looked doubtful, but he took a glass when the bartender filled it.

Ives touched his glass against McSween's and said, "Thanks, kid," nodding ever so slightly toward the cubbyhole. McSween's face thawed a little. Ives clinked silver on the bar and said loudly, "Time most of you boys got out on the street. Spread around and keep your eyes and ears open. I played that Long Nine ranny to get him to talk—and he did. Now we know that Frome's edgy. The question is: Will he really turn strangler? See what you can pick up. But a couple of you stay here and watch the front door."

They began moving out until only three were left. McSween put down his glass and started toward the door, walking steady for one with so much booze aboard.

Ives asked, "Where will you be if I want you, Joe?"

McSween's face had gone blank. "First I'm going to the store to get an armload of airtights. Then I'm heading south."

"That would be a lot of canned goods for a short ride, Joe."

McSween stepped out and closed the door behind him, making no answer to the implied question. Ives looked at the two who remained; they looked away from him. His anger rose again, but he told himself he mustn't let it show. McSween had made a royal fool of him, and the realization numbed his mind for a moment. Then he laughed. "No guts!" he said. "The kid's got no guts. I hope that talk about Long Nine's clean-up doesn't scare out the rest of you."

He turned toward the cubbyhole and let himself in. At first he saw only the bunk and table and chairs, and he almost called out her name in alarm and disappointment.

She was behind the door when he closed it, huddled tight and making herself small. "He saw my hat!" she whispered. "I heard all that talk out there! He saw my hat!"

He took her in his arms and drew her close. He felt her trembling. "Never you mind, honey."

"But suppose he tells Clem!"

"He won't. I scared him good, honey. He knows that I kept from shooting only because of you. These walls might not have stopped a stray forty-five slug."

She did not respond to his arms. He felt cheated; damned if this wasn't one more thing to lay at Loudon's door! She moved away and seated herself at the table. He took another of the chairs and propped it under the doorknob, then sat down across from her. "What you need is a drink, Addie. I can have the apron fetch us a bottle."

"You know I don't drink, Jack."

That was right, and it made him want to grin. She didn't mind cheating on her husband; but unlike some of the jades he'd known in the river towns, she wouldn't drink and she wouldn't smoke. She sat there pushing her black hair awry with nervous fingers. Scared though she was, her lips were full and her eyes were pretty. Damn pretty! Give her ten years, Ives reflected, and she'd be running to fat, with her face taking on a doughy look. But right now she stirred him deeply. He covered one of her hands with his. "Forget about it," he urged.

She said, "It's been horrible, waiting and listening to the talk. Is Frome really going to hit at you badlanders?"

"I'll take care of Frome," he said.

She shivered. "I think he'll be a hard man if he sets himself to it."

He hadn't come here to talk about Frome, but he supposed he'd have to let her run on till she got hold of herself. She was cold ashes now.

"I've never understood Frome," she said. "He comes to the place often; we put up hay for Long Nine, you know. When Clem's there, Frome's brief and all business. But when I'm alone, Jack, he stays an hour at a time. Just talking."

Ives looked at her sharply. "Talking about what?"

She shrugged. "Weather, and beef prices, and graze. The things men talk about. Sometimes he speaks of the school he'd like to start. He asked me if I'd be interested in teaching. He thought I'd be wonderful with children and wanted to know why Clem and I never had any. It's not what he talks about, Jack. It's the fact that he stays to talk when there are a hundred things that might be taking up his time."

He asked casually, "Has he ever tried making love to you?"

This startled her. "No, Jack. Of course not."

"I wonder—" Ives said and let it go at that. All this about Frome was something to be stored away for possible future use. Then he caught Addie Latcher's expression. She was dreaming, a strange speculation bright in her eyes.

She said, "That big house, and no woman in it . . ."

He was suddenly jealous. He told himself that this was crazy. He knew what he wanted from Addie Latcher. Hell, he'd never fooled himself about that. She was a constant warmth in his thoughts, and sometimes the remembrance of her brought him out of his blankets at night and set him pacing. After that he would find himself scouting Latcher's place in a fever of impatience. That fever was hot now, but there always had to be these preludes; he had to make small talk first and then turn it romantic for her; he had to make her think it was real as book and bell. His hand tightened on hers, and he said, "Addie—?"

Her mind was still far afield, and fear was back in her eyes again. "Jack," she said. "I wouldn't want Clem to know about us."

"He won't, honey."

"But Jess is a sort of friend of his. What will Jess do, Jack?"

Her talk brought him a picture of that moment in the other room when Loudon had walked out free, only to leave behind some strange pull that had taken Joe McSween away. Ives was remembering Loudon's saying, "You need any gear for a long ride, you come to me." He'd had two reasons for wanting Loudon dead, and now Addie had given him a third. Let Clem Latcher hear of these meetings, and he'd be keeping his woman under key.

Ives said, "I'll shut up Loudon. Soon. There'll be a time and a place. Damn him, no man crosses me the way he did!"

"You be careful, Jack!"

He wanted no more of this fretful talk. Not with the fever growing in him. Her hand moved in his; her hand was warm. He rose and came around behind her chair and bent and kissed her. Her lips responded; he could feel her need leap to meet his own.

He said hoarsely, "It's been a long time," and lifted her from the chair into his arms . . .

The Bower girl was asleep against Loudon's shoulder as he drove the buggy through the darkness toward the distant lights of Long Nine. He'd held himself stiffly for a long time, not wanting to disturb her.

He was mighty glad to see home ahead. He hadn't got any fun out of that hotel meal they'd eaten at Craggy Point; and a couple of times since, the girl had wondered aloud why Frome hadn't met her. He'd only grunted for answer. He'd got too tired for small talk, and Elizabeth Bower hadn't had much to say since sundown, either. Maybe that kiss had made them both feel awkward ever since. Now that had been a damn' fool thing to do! Let her tell Frome about it, and Jess Loudon would likely be down there at Miles City with Joe McSween, trying to hook up with one of those drovers. A fine howdy-you-do that would be, considering how all his ambitions were tied up with Frome.

He came into the ranch-yard near midnight, and the dogs were at once out and making racket. Light stood in the big house and, dimly, in the bunkhouse, too. But when he hauled on the reins before the wagon shed, he saw that the corral was nearly empty, and this surprised him and gave him an uneasy feeling.

Elizabeth came awake and looked around, startled. "Why, we're here!" she said.

Loudon got out and helped her down; she almost fell when she took the first step. A man's boots sounded against the hard-packed earth of the yard, and Ollie Scoggins shaped up.

Scoggins said, "Welcome back to Long Nine, Elizabeth."

The girl looked this way and that. "Where is my uncle, Ollie?"

Scoggins said, "Best come to the house. I've been keeping the coffeepot warm."

They moved away together. Loudon got the horse out of harness and put him into a barn stall and fed him. He walked back to the buggy and lifted the leather-bound trunk to his shoulder. The Winchester he left in the buggy. The rifle made him think of Scoggins. Mighty close-mouthed with the girl, Scoggins had been.

Loudon crossed over to the house and went inside, into the big parlor with its fireplace and fancy furniture and all the books. Had Frome really read all those books, or did he keep them just for show? The girl was deep in one of the chairs, nursing a coffee mug, and Scoggins was standing before the empty fireplace, his hands clasped behind him.

Loudon asked, "Where do I put this trunk?"

Scoggins waved in the direction of the spare bedroom, and Loudon took the trunk in there and set it down. When he came back into the parlor, Scoggins had coffee poured for him.

Scoggins was talking to the girl. "—built the new wing last fall. You'll find a lot of other changes in the place. It's the biggest in these parts."

Elizabeth said, very directly, "This trip my uncle took—Just when do you expect him back?"

"Tomorrow, maybe." Scoggins looked a mite embarrassed. He was a tall, stooped man, like a pine tree that had been hit too hard by the winds. He had the prairie squint and the wind-grooved face this country gave a man. He was an old saddle, Loudon thought, a little worn at the edges but still dependable. No, he was an old gun, made of blued steel and time-faded walnut but needing somebody to point him.

Elizabeth said, "It must be very important business that took my uncle away at the time of my coming."

"He had to go to Miles and palaver with the Stockgrowers' Association," Scoggins said. "It wouldn't keep."

Elizabeth nodded. "Mr. Loudon told me something of the trouble."

Scoggins frowned at Loudon, but when the foreman spoke, it was to Elizabeth. "Trouble enough," he admitted. "Maybe this wasn't a very good time for you to come."

"Mr. Loudon seemed inclined to that notion, too," she said.

Now it was coming, Loudon thought, but she only smiled. He guessed it was fun for her, having him on the hook and squirming. He emptied his coffee cup and set it down, giving her her chance if she was of a mind to tell about the kiss. He looked at her and said, "If that's all, I'm heading for the bunkhouse."

He nodded a goodnight and went out into the yard. The sky was black, and heat still clung to the earth. One of the dogs came up and sniffed at Loudon, then begged to be petted. He spoke softly, and the dog padded after him as he crossed to the buggy and lifted out the rifle. He strode to the bunkhouse and came inside to find one lamp burning, but the bunkhouse was empty.

He put the Winchester on the rifle rack and saw that the rack had been stripped of guns. Again he got that uneasy feeling.

Mighty plain that nobody had slept in the bunks tonight. The table holding the lamp had cards spread upon it and poker chips helter-skelter. On another table was the cribbage board and a scattering of magazines. A great one for keeping his crew in reading material, Peter Frome. He saw the unfinished hackamore Charley Fuller had been so patiently working on evenings. It brought him a clear picture of Charley and all the others, old and young, who rode for Long Nine. He was mighty near certain what had taken them out into the night.

It's come, he thought.

He walked about at first, and then, needing something for his hands to do, he got a magazine and turned the lamp wick higher and sat down. He was thumbing the pages, not really reading, when he heard Scoggins tramping the yard.

Scoggins came in and closed the door. "Not bedded down yet, eh?"

"I figured you'd be along to talk."

Scoggins frowned. "Did you have to tell her about the trouble?"

"Hell, it wouldn't have stayed a secret very long."

"I suppose not. Jess, it's sure come to a head."

Loudon put down the magazine. "I thought so."

"Skinny Egan rode in this afternoon. You remember those Idaho horses Frome had up at the head of Prickly? The whole kit and kaboodle got moved out in the dark of the moon. A week ago, maybe. Skinny followed the sign as far as it led, which was straight toward the badlands. But the sign was pretty old. Ives' bunch, Jess."

"Again?"

"Frome talked to me before he left. He figgers we got to start the clean-up. Pronto. He's gone to make sure the Stockgrowers' will back us up all the way. He said if anything happened while he was gone, I should use my own judgment. Well, it happened."

"And you used your judgment?"

"I did some studying on it. Then I sent the crew out tonight. All of 'em. To look for Ives' bunch."

"Which direction?"

"Up Prickly."

Loudon said, "Then all they'll get out of it is sore butts. Ives had his whole outfit at Craggy Point this afternoon. And if you send the boys to Craggy tomorrow, Ives will likely be back on the Prickly."

"How would *you* do it, Jess?"

"Same as you, I guess. You want me riding tonight?"

Scoggins shook his head. "You've put in a mighty full day. Frome told me to give you the job of going after her. He sets quite a store by you, Frome does. Elizabeth said you gave her a good trip. Better get to bed."

"Sure," Loudon said.

Scoggins turned toward the door. "Damn it, but this will be a mean business!"

Loudon looked at him and thought that even a pine tree sometimes got bent till it broke. He'd seen them bowled over with the jagged stump showing, the wood washed brown by the rain. He said, "There's only one answer to this rustling. Frome knows it. You know it. I know it."

Scoggins nodded and left; Loudon heard the dwindling beat of his boots. He got up and wondered if he should go to the cook-shack and get himself a can of tomatoes. But he could wait for breakfast. He loosened his belt and dug into his pockets and began spilling their contents on the table. He brought out the five dollars Joe McSween had given him and stacked them neatly. He sat down and began tugging at one of his boots, his bones weary, his mind fuzzy. And then it hit him.

"Good God! Joe!" he thought, and found that he'd said it aloud.

He stood up, shaken. He looked around this bunkhouse, knowing where his loyalty lay. But those five dollars still gleamed on the table. He picked them up and dumped them back into his pocket. Then he bent and blew out the lamp and headed for the corral to get himself a saddle horse. He was running when he reached the gate.

4

Red Eye Burning

IN THE DARK, GETTING READY TO RIDE WAS A CHORE. He stood in the corral wasting loops, trying to hang one on his own horse, the horse he had paid out his good wages to get. He supposed anxiety was making him wooden handed, and he was stirring up considerable commotion. He kept looking toward the house where Ollie Scoggins was bedded down; he kept expecting Ollie to come and ask what the hell was going on. He wouldn't have any answer that would make sense to Scoggins.

His loop filled then, and his black gelding began to lead out from the other horses. His saddle had been knocked from the top of the corral, and the fleece lining took some brushing to get the dirt out. This done, Loudon saddled and bridled quickly and got out of the corral. He rode halfway across the yard before he turned back, knowing what he might need but not letting himself really believe it. He stepped down before the open door of the blacksmith shop, which was also the tool shed. Inside, he spent a few matches and rummaged about till he found a short-handled shovel. He brought this out and tied it to the saddle, the horse shying. Then Loudon lifted himself to the saddle again.

He cut away from the ranch, moving slow so as not to fuss the dogs. He headed northwest and hipped around once for a look back. The white frame ranch-house stood spooky and shapeless. Frome's house.

Ollie Scoggins had said tonight that Frome set quite a store by him. That had been a surprise. He remembered the day he'd first ridden to Long Nine and asked for a job. Frome had put a lot of questions to him. Pointless questions they'd seemed, some of them, but afterwards he'd realized he'd told Frome just about everything about his backtrail and how he stood on this matter and that. He remembered Frome standing at the top of the porch steps; he'd wondered how tall Frome was, it being hard to tell with Frome up there. He'd never really found out if Frome was taller than himself. A man couldn't go sidling up to Frome to take his measure.

Then there were those first weeks when he'd ridden with the crew, finding Long Nine's boys eager enough to teach him the ropes but kind of holding off from him as though they weren't yet of a mind whether he was wolf or dog. Probably they'd heard he'd partnered with Joe McSween, and they knew that Joe had since tied up with Idaho Jack Ives. But they hadn't held that against Jess Loudon in the long run. He could get the makings from any of them, or the price of a drink or a pair of California pants, if he was caught between pay days. But tonight the crew was riding for one reason and he for another.

At first he moved straight across country, heading toward the Prickly. He wished the moon could get through that smoke pall. By straining his eyes hard, he could make out a far rim of low hills, but mostly he traveled by memory, and he traveled at a trot though the cry in him was to gallop.

Damn a country that had a level feel to it but was peppered with potholes that would make a horse fall! Here you had bunchgrass, but those sunken spots were all around, just as they were in the badlands to the north up along the Missouri. Funny thing about badlands country, it had no real beginning or end. You'd call this good grazing country, figuring the badlands were somewhere beyond; yet the badlands were here, too, not stony and sculptured and plain to see but sort of edging into the prairie. And there were washouts, and coulees thick with chokeberry bushes; and if you didn't mind your riding, your horse would be down with a broken leg.

Loudon sighed. All he could do was push on carefully. No sense even wasting a match to cut sign on the Long Nine crew. They might be riding in aimless circles, hunting the night.

No, the job was to put himself in Joe McSween's boots and figure out where he'd go if he were Joe. He got trying to think what Joe was really like, going over all the jumble of remembering for some small sign that would tell him where Joe would be tonight. He kept remembering their frolicking in Miles City, and campfires shared, and Joe's grin so warm and ready, and bottles drained down to the last drop. But what about something important, such as whether Joe would have pushed on, set on making Miles as soon as possible? Or whether he'd have spread out his blankets somewhere and now be sleeping sound?

Studying on it, Loudon realized that Joe had never been in any special hurry to get anywhere. Slow as a stump, Joe, except when he was riled. Come time to make camp, Loudon judged, and Joe would have found a creek with some trees around. Scrub cedar grew up at the head of Prickly, and here and there a cottonwood. Loudon didn't like thinking about the cottonwoods.

His horse shied violently, almost throwing him. He pressed his knees hard against the saddle. Something went skittering away in the night. An antelope, Loudon guessed. Nothing to get jumpy about, but he was sticky under the arms and as edgy as a bear with cubs. He minded his riding more carefully, and soon he came upon the Prickly, a sluggish stream this dry season, its water red with gumbo.

Loudon began following the creek upstream, the land rising gently and not putting any real strain on the horse. Presently he was atop a hogback ridge, and here he paused and had a look around. Back toward the Long Nine buildings, the land he'd crossed was a lake of darkness. No light showed at the ranch. In the other direction, the ragged hills rose, humpy against the sky. He knew then how many miles he'd covered and guessed that it was getting on toward dawn.

Leaning forward in the saddle, he listened hard. He wondered if Long Nine rode in a bunch and if the strike of many hoofs on gravelly ground might carry to him. He heard nothing. And then he saw a single red eye burning higher up in the hills, and his fear rose again and choked him.

That would be no campfire of Joe McSween's. It was too late at night or too early in the morning for a campfire. That blaze had been built by those who needed light for a job to do; and knowing this, his arm ached to lash his horse to a high gallop, but the terrain here was even more uncertain than it had been below. He could only move forward at a walk, heading on toward that red beacon and feeling space around him like a wall that wouldn't budge to his shoving.

Before he'd covered a mile, the fire winked out. Now there was nothing to do but ride on upward, hanging hard to the hope that the fire hadn't meant what he'd thought. Yet he knew what he'd find when he reached the spot. He'd known from the first, when he fetched the shovel.

All his thinking became gray. He could turn back now, he reflected, for maybe Long Nine had done that shovel job. But in him was some urge to see this thing through. He was moving entirely by feel. Finally, he got down and led the gelding as the pitch turned steeper. His ankles hurt, and his boots rubbed. He was into scrub cedar. He wanted more than anything else in the world to sit down on a deadfall and let time run on, but he kept moving.

Once he came alert, sure that he heard the crashing of horses through timber over on the far bank of the Prickly. That would be Long Nine heading homeward. He could have called out and got the answer to the question that ached in him, but the crew would ask questions in turn, questions he couldn't answer any more than he could have answered Ollie Scoggins. Yet he felt odd, hiding from them like an enemy. Damn it, he was Long Nine, too! But there was the memory of Joe McSween's smile.

No, he told himself, there was nothing to do but keep moving upward. He tried hard to hold in his mind that spot where the fire had burned; and nearing it, he moved in circles, hunting, hunting.

He grew sore with tiredness, and his mind began playing him tricks. He heard voices and pulled up short, knowing there could be no voices. Then he realized it was the Prickly splashing over stones. He moved on, his feet dragging, and suddenly the horse snorted and reared back, pulling hard at the reins in his hand. He looked up and saw something black and shapeless turning gently above him, turning ever so gently . . .

"No!" he said. "No!"

Afterwards he didn't remember much about getting Joe McSween down, except that it was a devil of a job. He struck just one match. He'd seen dead men before, plenty of them, but none that had been hanged, and none that was Joe.

No, death was an old graybeard in a pine box, with a preacher standing over him making talk of pearly gates, while the womenfolk stood around sniffling and everybody spoke hushed, no matter how much of a hellion the man in the box might have been. Or death was a man gone down in a stampede or lost in a wild river crossing or dropped by a bullet in some saloon fracas. Death was something that crept up on the old or struck fast at the young, but it wasn't a rope over a tree limb and a saddle bucketing out from under a man. A lynching was death without dignity.

He straightened Joe out and supposed he should put a blanket over him. He had no more feeling in him than Joe had, no hate and no anger, but only a tired numbness. This was like getting hit by a bullet. You waited for the pain.

Dawn light began to show in the east, and this stirred Loudon to action. He went over to where Long Nine had built the fire; there was space for his purpose among the trees. He got the shovel and went to work with it. Only when he began pushing the loose dirt back into the hole was he struck by his first sense of complete reality, knowing then that in all the night's riding he had clung hard to a hope that had ended here. He scrounged about till he'd picked up enough rocks to cover the mound. He kicked the shovel aside and found himself with nothing left to do.

He supposed Joe's horse was around somewhere.

But that horse would get along by itself from here on out, and the saddle was nobody's now. Loudon climbed aboard his own horse. Maybe a man should say a few words over the mound, but no words came, only the harsh thinking, the wondering.

How did you face up to them, Joe? No begging and whining, I'll bet, because you didn't live that way, and you sure as hell wouldn't have died that way!

He put his back to that lone cottonwood and rode through the scrub cedar, which was now filtered with gray; he rode slack, without destination, until finally it came to him that he couldn't go back to Long Nine. Not now. This, too, left him with a sense of loss. Picking his way downhill, he headed north by east. He wanted something, and he was riding toward it, but he couldn't have given it a name. Not till much later did he realize that he wanted to be with the one person who could share his grief. He was going to Craggy Point and Ike Nicobar because there was no other medicine in the world for what ailed him.

5

Elizabeth

AWAKENING, ELIZABETH BOWER FELT UNUTTERABLY alone. She lay on a tick stuffed with sweetgrass; she could see the curtains moving idly at the window, and the room was very peaceful. Yet she felt depressed. She threw aside the covers and tried with the gesture to throw aside her mood.

She would plan her day at once, and it would include riding. Two years ago Scoggins had taught her how to stay aboard a stock saddle. She'd packed a wide skirt in the trunk Jess Loudon had fetched last night. Opening the trunk, she thought of Loudon, remembering his wild talk aboard the *Prairie Belle,* remembering his rough kiss. She called up a clear picture of him, tall and loose legged, his face sun darkened. An eagle's face? No, Loudon was more like a hawk wheeling high and remote. But his mouth had a curve of generosity.

She used pitcher and bowl, washing with cold water. She was dressing when voices came from the big, outer room, a rumble of half-heard words. When one of the voices rose, she recognized it as Scoggins'. Then she realized with sharp surprise that the other speaker was Frome, and she said his name in her mind. *Frome.* She'd never thought of him by any other name. He'd not been Uncle Peter to her, even in her childhood days. But she'd really not known him then, having only a hazy remembrance of a big man with a deep voice. When she had come out here two years ago, it had been like visiting a stranger who was somehow kin.

That was why she hadn't faced up to him then about the shadow that lay between them. But this time she was determined that they would talk it out. Was that why she had awakened depressed, knowing the hour to be near? *Get it done,* she thought. *Get it done and behind you.*

She finished dressing and made her bed. She looked at the yard from her window, glimpsing a corner of the bunk-house. There seemed to be no great activity about the place; the ranch lay hushed, somber as the smoky sky overhead. Ollie Scoggins passed across her range of vision, heading toward the corrals. Knuckles beat against her bedroom door, and she swung about.

Frome asked, "Are you up, my dear?"

"Yes," she called and opened the door.

He advanced and embraced her; his lips just brushed her cheek. He stood back and held her at arm's length, then placed his big hands at her waist and lifted her from the floor and set her down. He said in his deep, remembered voice, "You've grown up, girl. Sorry I couldn't be at the Point to meet you yesterday. Business. Come have some breakfast. Had mine early—drove most of the night. But I could use another cup of coffee."

He'd been a big man always, and though he was

running a little to paunch, he was stately, she decided. He wore a black suit, with a gold watch chain stretched across his vest. With that massive head and those strong, clean-cut features, he could have been a Roman senator, except for the full mustache, so inky black, half hiding his mouth. He led her through the house toward the kitchen.

"See," he said with a flourish of his hand. "A bigger house than you remember, I'll bet. Do you like the bow windows? And the leaded panes? Had them freighted overland." Into the kitchen, he seated her at the table. Then he stepped to the back door, cupped his hands to his mouth, and bellowed in the direction of the cook shack, "Sam!"

Two years ago he'd taken his meals in the cook shack, and so had she. Now that the house had been enlarged, there was room in the kitchen for a big round table. She was going to miss eating with the crew.

Frome took a chair across from her and smiled fondly. "Ollie says you fetched only a small trunk. We'll get you more clothes at Miles City. Do you remember Orschel's store? They'll rig you out properly. You'll be staying on here, girl."

She didn't like his stating how it would be instead of asking, and she felt her rebellion rise. Sam, the cook, came through the doorway and shook hands with her gravely, then moved to the stove. He'd carried in a bowl of flapjack batter. Shortly he served her and poured coffee for Frome as well. Frome said, "You can go along, Sam. I'll call you if you're needed." All this while Frome had been leaning back in his chair, studying her. Now he watched while she ate. She felt he was pressing her, even with his silence. Was he thinking of the shadow, too?

At last he said, "You look like your father's side of the house. I can see Jonathan Bower in you. I'm wondering if you think as he did."

Now it's coming, she thought, and she began to tremble inside and willed herself not to show this. *Get it done,* she had told herself, but she had supposed she'd be the one to open the subject.

He took a drink of his coffee and drew the back of his hand across his mustache. "Your father never liked me. I think you know why. I suppose I should have explained to you two years ago, but I never quite got to it. I want nothing between us, Elizabeth. That's why I'm talking now. I expect you know that when your grandfather Frome died, his property went solely to me. Your mother supposed I'd divide with her; we'd had that understanding. But I liquidated the property, pocketed the cash, and went west."

She said stiffly, "I was a small girl then. I heard my mother's side of the story."

He frowned. "So I appeared selfish. I can only tell you now that I intended to make amends when I got established."

"I'm afraid that didn't help my mother much, or my father," she said. "They both stayed bitter about you till they died."

His face hardened. "If it's any consolation to you, the money didn't last long in the gold camps of Virginia City and Confederate Gulch. I worked with pick and shovel and went hungry and slept cold. A small strike gave me a new stake. I might have sent your mother her half, but by then I'd got hold of a real idea. I could see that the future of the Territory was going to be cattle, not gold. I went searching for graze and finally found this spot. The first couple of years I worked here alone till I could afford a crew." He spread out his big hands, palms upward, so that the callouses showed. "Look," he said. "Did I have it easy?"

She sat rigid. "And now—?" she asked.

"And now I see a future here, not only for myself but for many people." He came to his feet, swept upward by his own enthusiasm. "I see towns rising. I see churches and schools. The fact is, Elizabeth, I'm planning a school. There are children at several of the ranches. And whatever I do will have started from the money I fetched from Ohio. Remember that when you judge me."

She said, truly surprised, "Why, you're asking forgiveness!"

He shook his head. "No, girl. All I want is your understanding. You're the only kin I have. Everything I build will belong to you, including such honor as I can bring to my name. If it can be said that I robbed your mother, then I robbed you. Now I can make amends. That's why I want you to stay on here."

So you can appease your conscience! The thought was hot in her, and she wanted to fling it at him, but she couldn't bring herself to it. Not when he stood like a sad and harmless bear. Yet in her was no sure knowledge of him, and that was where her need lay. She had hoped to truly know him two years ago, but the visit had been too short. But still the need had persisted, and it had brought her across the miles again.

He had turned and was staring out the window, his hands clasped behind him. She rose, too. "I'll stay," she said. "But it's only fair to warn you that I'll be watching you. I think I have the right to ask the proof of your honesty."

She glimpsed his face then, mirrored in the window, and for an instant it was savage, or was that merely a natural tightening of his lips brought on by her bluntness? As he turned about, his look was angry but held no threat. "Fair enough," he said. "Perhaps I deserve less." He moved toward the back door. "I've got work to do. You'll want something, too, I suppose. You can teach at the school when I get it ready."

He went out, and she leaned against the wall. Teach school? Be another instrument in his hand? Yet it was not the selfish men who built schools. She must not judge one way or the other; she must not judge. Not yet. But she felt as though she had just come through a hard fight and didn't know whether she had emerged the victor. She felt weak from the effort spent.

After awhile she went out into the yard.

Frome was riding away, two men with him, the three walking their horses to the northwest with Frome looking clumsy in the saddle. Elizabeth watched him and then gazed about, trying to feel come home. But the bunkhouse was larger now, and there were several new outbuildings, so that Long Nine was like a person she'd known who'd grown up overnight and become half a stranger. No, the change was even greater than that; it came from a difference in atmosphere. Too quiet—too utterly quiet. Some of the crew lolled around the bunkhouse, and there was activity near the corrals, but everyone seemed to be speaking softly and stepping softly.

Scoggins came across the yard, and she wished him good morning. He looked tired. "Will you saddle up for me, Ollie?" she asked. "A gentle horse. I'm out of practice."

"Where you riding?"

"Toward Latcher's."

"I don't think you'd better, Elizabeth."

"Why not?"

He hesitated, and then his words came with a rush. "That trouble we mentioned got started last night.

The boys caught a rustler and hung him. They figgered to leave him dangling as a warning to others. That didn't set with Frome. He's gone to cut him down and give him proper burying."

Something smote her hard as a fist. The reality of what Jess Loudon had tried to tell her was here, filling the world. She looked at Scoggins and felt angry with him, needing her anger to hang onto. Couldn't he have found a kinder way to tell her? But when she saw the trouble in his face, she knew he'd used the only words he could command.

He said, almost pleading, "You don't understand. It had to be done, Elizabeth."

"I still want to go riding," she said. "Ollie, I've got to get out where I can think."

"Then one of the boys better ride with you."

"Jess Loudon?"

Scoggins shrugged. "He rode out somewheres last night. He ain't come back."

"Last night? But it was so late!"

Scoggins nodded. "I know. It don't make sense. Or maybe it does. The fellow that got hung got riding with Idaho Jack Ives and his badlanders. Out here a man's apt to be one side of the fence or the other. Before that, this fellow was a buffalo hunter. He partnered with old Ike Nicobar and with Jess. They were pretty close, Jess and Joe McSween."

Elizabeth shook her head. Somehow it made the dead man a person, his having a name. Now she could begin to wonder if he'd been fat or lean, gay or sad, and who his people were. But it was Jess she was really thinking about—Jess, who had been the dead man's friend. Odd how small your own troubles were when you looked at somebody else's. She said, "I'll ride alone. I'll run for home if anyone shows."

He turned toward the corral. "I don't know as

Frome will like this." But he saddled for her, picking out a little paint that looked fleet, and he fetched her a pair of spurs.

She thanked him when she climbed aboard the horse. Scoggins' eyes showed no enthusiasm. She was being stubborn again, she knew, the way she'd been when Jess Loudon had tried to persuade her to stay aboard the packet.

She rode northward into the vast emptiness. She rode slowly, sometimes looking back at the ranch buildings growing small with distance, sometimes looking toward the three diminutive riders heading for the Prickly. Her thoughts became a jumble of Frome and Jess Loudon and the harsh news Scoggins had delivered.

Across the last two years she'd remembered the land not as savage in its sweep but friendly. There was a place in the badlands to which she'd often ridden to search for petrified fish and sea shells; and Frome had explained to her that once, ages ago, all this land was under water. She'd promised herself that she would go back to that place the very first day, but now the nearing rim of the badlands repelled her. She felt cheated and sickened, and in her grew an impulse to hurry back to Ohio and its safety.

Yet she'd come West this second time half-intending to stay. She had intended to make her full decision after she'd got here and had it out with Frome about that old business of the inheritance. Beyond the need to know the truth about that had been her hope that he would measure up. That settled, she would know her future.

But the doing of last night was Frome's doing, really. By his orders a man had died. Still, lawlessness had to be punished. The trouble—no fault of Frome's —was that the day hadn't come to Montana when such punishment could be meted out in the proper way. Of course! In Ohio she had read in the paper of executions, but she hadn't found herself having breakfast with the hangman. That was the real difference. But Frome rode now to leaven a necessary evil with kindness.

With such thinking, she felt less horrified; and the land began to look brighter, its old beauty showing again. She had been more than an hour on the trail, and Long Nine's buildings were out of sight when she looked back. The land had been dipping gently toward the Missouri. West of Craggy Point, the river looped southward, she remembered, and at the bottom of that sweeping curve sat Latcher's hay ranch. Thus the distance was nowhere nearly so great from Long Nine to Latcher's as it was from Long Nine to Craggy Point, and within another hour she was riding down into the breaks with Latcher's place below her. There were the house and the log stable and corral, a little garden patch, and on the flat nearby several stacks of good bluejoint hay, wire-corraled to fend off stock.

Shortly she rode up to Latcher's fence and dismounted. She looped the reins over the gate post and walked toward the log house.

She'd come here, she supposed, merely because it had made a destination. What little she'd seen of Clem Latcher on that other trip west she'd liked. About Addie, she wasn't sure. She could sit and drink coffee with Addie by the hour and find her hungry for tidbits from the outside world; but there'd been no bridging to Addie, really.

Remembering this, Elizabeth told herself she would make the visit short. And just then she heard sobbing. The sound stopped her. She stood at one corner of the house, beside a wood pile cut from the cottonwoods along the river. She stood close enough that she might have put out a hand to the silvered siding. The sobbing was so plain that she knew a window must be open. It was Addie crying. Elizabeth heard Clem Latcher's voice then, sharp and impatient and bitter. "You've got to tell me his name, Addie. I'll keep asking till you do."

"What good would that do?"

"Don't you understand? I'm not blaming you. I'm blaming him for taking advantage of you."

Addie sobbed again. "I'll never go back to him."

"Oh, yes, you will. You know you will. He was someone who was in Craggy Point yesterday. Was it Jack Ives?"

"Clem, we've been at this for hours!"

"McSween?"

"No!"

"Jess Loudon? Now that I think about it, it could have been."

Panic choked Elizabeth. This was like coming upon someone undressed. She looked back toward the gate. Her horse was pointing its ears at the corral where a couple of horses switched lazily at flies. In a moment the paint would nicker. She turned and fled. She untied the reins from the gate post and led the horse at a careful walk for a good hundred yards. Then she swung to the saddle and began the climb up from the river bottom.

On the flat land above, she rode south slowly through the late afternoon, trying to shut her mind to what she had heard. But still Addie's sobbing stayed in her ears, and Latcher's bitter voice. She felt sorry for both of them, and she hoped they hadn't heard her and come looking. Might it not have been better if she'd gone on around and knocked at the door?

She mustn't think about it—today had been bad, first with Frome bringing up the thing between them, and then Ollie Scoggins blurting out about the hanging. And now—this. She had got nothing from this ride but more trouble; and when she came upon a coulee, she dipped down into it and followed along, liking the aloneness here. There were a lot of these coulees cutting across the land and not showing until you were upon them. Bushes grew here.

Soon she heard cattle bawling. Scoggins had told her two years ago how the coulees had to be combed at roundup time; and when she came upon the cattle, perhaps twenty in all, she noticed first that they wore the Long Nine brand and that the calves were unbranded. Some remnant of the herd, overlooked in spring roundup? But how would the cowhands have missed so many? She drew rein and stared at the cattle, puzzled.

She didn't see the man until he was almost upon her. She heard a horse break through brush, and when she looked up, startled, the man was there. He drew alongside her, a youngish fellow dressed like a working cowhand. "Who would you be, miss?" he asked.

She decided she didn't like him; he had a mean eye and his smile was too thin. "I'm Frome's niece, from Long Nine," she said. "I don't remember you. Are you new to the crew?" But now she noticed the brand on his horse, and it wasn't Long Nine.

He reached out a hand to lay it on her arm. "Why don't you light down for a spell," he said. "We'll talk things over."

She knew then. This man was a rustler, hidden out where he could keep an eye on these cattle! Come dark, he'd be drifting them on toward the badlands, holding them at such way stations as this while the sun was up. Spying her, he had showed himself out of curiosity; and now he had to keep her till these cattle were moved. She jerked her arm away and gave the spur to her horse. She swung the horse hard against his and struck at the man with her quirt. He fell from the saddle, shouting with surprise and anger.

Two more riders came out of the brush of the coulee's slope. One of these was range garbed, the other wore black and was tall and pinch waisted. The man on the ground shouted, "Get her, damn it! She's had a good look at me!"

Wheeling her horse about, Elizabeth spurred hard. When she looked back, the man she had unhorsed was pulling himself to the saddle, and then all three were coming on after her. The cows blocked their way. Elizabeth laid her quirt against the paint. The horse stumbled and almost went down. She got beyond the cattle and held her mount to a gallop. A gun sounded, and another. She realized then how truly desperate her situation was. They couldn't let her get away. Not now. She got to the end of the coulee and rode out of it onto the prairie.

South! her mind screamed at her. South to Long Nine and safety; but when she looked over her shoulder again, the three were out of the coulee and had fanned wide and were cutting her off from heading south.

"Come back, girl!" one shouted. "Come back, and you won't be hurt!"

Now she was in the open where the paint could really stretch his legs, and she blessed Ollie Scoggins for picking a horse so fleet. They were herding her to the north and the east, but she was gaining on them, and they wouldn't dare hold to this chase long. Not with Craggy Point to the northeast, and somewhere near she would intersect the wagon road with its possibility of traffic. But they were shooting again. She guessed that they were trying to scare her into stopping or drop her horse, one of the two. Then something struck her shoulder heavy as a hammer, and she was almost driven over the horse's head.

She lost one rein as she clutched hard at the horn. She rode on knowing that she'd been hit, knowing that she would fall from the saddle soon.

6

A Man's Choice

HE WAS, JESS LOUDON REALIZED, A MAN CUT LOOSE FROM everything. He sat here in the little office of the livery stable, Ike Nicobar with him and talking, but a lot of the time he wasn't really listening to Ike. He'd hear Ike's voice, but his mind would go away and deep into thinking and then come back. He'd got here in early morning and told Ike the news about Joe McSween and then climbed into the hay loft and slept. He'd slept most of the day. When he'd come down the ladder, Ike had fetched him something to eat. There was a bottle on the bench between them, but he'd let Ike do the drinking. There were no good answers in the bottom of a bottle that Jess Loudon had ever found.

"Ye mind that time we rode the packet to St. Louis," Ike was saying. "Joe poured himself a drink of river water, and ye could have dropped an egg in the glass and never found it; it was that muddy. Remember, Jess? Joe swore he'd live on whiskey the rest of the trip. And he did."

Loudon ran a hand across his cheeks and jaw. Rough . . . He needed shaving or currying, one of the two. He looked at his hand and saw the dirt imbedded under his fingernails, and that took him back to the digging job he'd done last night. A little thing could bring all the memory rushing. He'd think that he was getting used to the idea of Joe gone, and then the whole thing would hit him again.

"He was born for trouble, that Joe," Nicobar was going on. "Ye recollect that night out of Yankton on that same steamboat? Joe took on a load of busthead and started walking the railing of the boiler deck. Flappin' his arms like a rooster's wings and crowin', and me and you beggin' him to get down before he tumbled into the river and got sucked under into the wheel. Us not darin' to grab holt of him lessen he lost his balance. By God, he put feathers in my belly that night, Joe did!"

Loudon nodded. It all came back to him stark and scary, Joe teetering there on the railing and that old stern wheel a-pounding. Pemmican that paddle would have made of him if he'd gone overboard. Well, Joe hadn't tumbled, and he'd got a couple more years of living, only to end up with a rope around his neck. Was that better? Not by a damn' sight! Why couldn't Joe have had his light blown out that night aboard the steamboat? Why couldn't he have died full of liquor and fun, instead of the way it had finally happened?

Ike was talking about St. Louis now, and the spreeing they'd done there. Loudon's mind went away from Ike again. He thought of Ollie Scoggins, who'd been so worried last night, and he thought of Peter Frome, who had given the order, and of Idaho Jack Ives, who had led Joe too far along the wrong trail. His mind flitted to that girl he'd taken off the boat yesterday. Well, he'd tried to tell her what Long Nine would be like, but she hadn't believed. They didn't grow that kind of fruit on Ohio trees.

He shook his head. He couldn't put her down as feather-brained. There was something about her that stuck with him and bothered him. Not her saucy smile or the way she hadn't jabbed the spurs in him at the ranch—not telling about the kiss—but something deeper. Something that told him it was more than a whim that had taken her to Long Nine against his warning. Maybe she had worries, too; she'd kept asking why Frome hadn't met her. He got wondering about the girl and Frome, knowing they were kin, yet finding no likeness between them . . .

Ike had quit talking. He took a pull at the pint and drew his sleeve across his mouth. "Ye'd better be riding now, Jess," he said then. "It's a far piece to Long Nine and dark will be comin' on."

These words jarred through to Loudon. "Hell, Ike, I'm not going back there. Ever."

Nicobar said gently, "Joe's dead and gone, Jess."

"And who killed him?"

"Hark to me, Jess," Nicobar urged. "Yesterday you was saying that the man who's tied to a boss won't be drifting into trouble. Nothing's been changed since, except that what was bound to happen happened." His old face puckered. "Ye've still got to ask yourself whether you belong to Long Nine or the badlanders. Now which is it going to be?"

Loudon remembered that second sense of loss he'd had after he'd buried Joe, the loss that had come with knowing he couldn't go back to Long Nine. Not after what they'd done to Joe. Damn it, that was why he was feeling cut loose from everything now! He said, "You're forgetting, Ike, that I've slammed the door behind me. They'll figure out who buried Joe. Frome will read that as a sign as to how I stand."

"Maybe so," Nicobar said. "That still leaves ye with a choice to make. What you going to do?"

"Drift."

"Where ye driftin'?"

He hadn't given that any thought. There were those drovers at Miles City who were hiring hands. He could take the very advice he'd given Joe and sign up with one of them. But that would be like the buffalo hunting—far trails and new skylines each day, but a man standing still for all that he moved across the face of the world. Joe had said yesterday that Jess Loudon had always been ambitious. Being with a boss like Peter Frome was more than just being tied to something; it was the first long step toward being a man of Frome's cut and caliber. And that was what he wanted, really. If the ambition had to have a name, let the name be Frome. With Frome he'd have grown. Someday he might have been Frome's right hand, or even the owner of land of his own, a man like Frome that other men looked up to, a man who didn't stand still.

Face the truth! That's why he'd gone to Frome in the first place. He'd seen the changes coming with the buffalo hunting ended and fewer steamboats on the river and another railroad coming in. He'd told himself that if he didn't tie hard to something, he'd end up with the badlanders as Joe McSween had. But he'd been looking a lot farther ahead than just to next week or next season. He'd taken the first long step so as to ready himself for the second. But the thing that had spiked him on a sharp stick was Joe's being hung. He couldn't go and pat Frome on the back for that!

Where was he drifting, Ike had asked. That was the question. Back to the aimlessness he'd known most of his years? He reckoned not. On to some other ranch where at least he'd be tied to a boss? But that boss wouldn't be Peter Frome, and that made all the difference. Standing at the foot of those ranch-house steps, he'd wondered how tall Frome stood. He guessed he would never know another man as tall as Frome.

But still there was Joe McSween to remember.

"I'll ride around a while, Ike," he said. "I'll latch onto something."

He'd better be getting at it, too. He walked out of the office and began saddling his horse. Ike trailed along and stood watching. Loudon dug into his pocket for money and found silver dollars. But those dollars had been Joe's, so he dug into another pocket. He couldn't spend Joe's dollars. He couldn't give them back to Joe, either. He couldn't do a damn' thing but hang onto them. He laid one of his own dollars in Ike's hand. "That's for taking care of my horse, old timer."

Nicobar said, "Ye find another job now. Hear, boy?"

Loudon nodded, promising nothing. He led the horse outside and stepped up to the saddle. The afternoon was nearly gone, he judged; around him Craggy Point drowsed beneath the smoky sky. East lay the badlands; he rode west. He walked the horse along the street and was of a mind to follow the river upstream until he recalled that that would bring him to Latcher's hay ranch. Damned if he wanted to see Addie. He guessed she would always remind him of Jack Ives and so turn his thinking to Joe McSween. He reined to the left when the street became the wagon road and climbed the road to the crest of the breaks. He rode slowly south across the flat country then. It struck him that he was heading out along the very way Joe had taken the last time he'd seen Joe alive.

His mind was again working the way it had when he'd been in the livery office with Ike. He'd fall into thought and then he'd come back to his surroundings like a man waking from sleep, but mostly he was lost deep in himself. He'd think of anything in creation and the thought would work itself around to Joe McSween somehow, and the pain would rush through him again. Then he'd push the thinking away and look around him. Sometimes the road led past the bleached bones of buffalo; sometimes he glimpsed antelope on distant hogbacks. He'd have to turn off this road before many miles or he'd find himself at Long Nine's corral before he knew it.

Sound struck through to him. Shots! Those were shots!

He hauled on the reins and looked about. To the west he saw riders, one out ahead and three others spread behind the first. Smoke puffed from one of those three; the sound of the shot reached to Loudon, and then he recognized the pattern of flight and pursuit. What the hell was going on? The one pursued seemed to be having trouble. A rein was flying loose, and the rider swayed in the saddle, almost falling.

Neck-reining toward the four, Loudon touched spurs to his horse and galloped hard. He got his own gun out and held it ready. The distance closed fast; he saw that the pursued was a woman; he could make out the billowing skirt. Addie Latcher? He knew of no other woman who lived hereabouts. Then he realized it was the Bower girl.

He had no time to be surprised or to wonder what she was doing out here or why she was being chased. He fired; the shot was to tell those three he was buying in. He was still covering ground, and now he recognized the black-garbed figure among the pursuers. Ives! Anger beat in Loudon, and all this was suddenly personal—personal as it had been when he'd stood up to Ives in the Assiniboine yesterday. He shouted at the

Bower girl, "Over here!" and she made an attempt to swerve the horse. He was close enough now to see how white her face was.

He got to her and swung his horse around and leaned down and snatched that trailing rein. He had noticed an upthrust of rocks a few hundred yards to the north, a natural breastwork perhaps four feet high. Dragging at the rein, he hauled the girl's horse at a gallop toward those rocks.

Ives and the other two had pulled up short. They seemed undecided for a moment, not knowing quite how to play out this game now that it had taken a new turn. Ives shouted something, and all three gigged their mounts and came on again. But those few moments of respite had counted for Loudon. He got to the rocks and flung himself down from the saddle and shouted to the girl, "Get to cover!" She almost fell from the saddle. He moved quickly to help her and got her into his arms. He saw then that she was wounded. Blood showed dark against the fabric of her shirt.

"My shoulder," she said.

"Bad hurt?"

"I—I can't tell."

"No time to look at it," he said. "Here they come!"

He forced her to the ground behind the rocks. He rested the barrel of his gun carefully upon his crooked left arm. Those three were looming up big and bigger. He picked Ives as his target, but even as he fired he knew he'd missed. He fired three times in quick succession then, not really aiming but just hoping to discourage the charge. One of Ives' men lurched in his saddle, then jerked at the reins, veering his horse away. Ives and the other man turned back.

Loudon fired once again and then bobbed behind the rocks and punched fresh cartridges into his gun. He glanced at the girl. She was crouched down, staring at him. He peered over the top of the rocks. Ives and his friends had withdrawn beyond pistol range and now were huddled together, talking. The one Loudon had wounded seemed to be shaking his head. Loudon watched them closely.

"Here they come again," he told Elizabeth.

But only two were making the charge—Ives and the other unwounded man. They came at a gallop; they came firing. Lead splintered the tops of the rocks and ricocheted, whining. Loudon risked standing and laid several shots fast. He scored no hits, but again he broke the charge. Both men wheeled about, riding back and rejoining the third man. Again they talked, Ives waving his arm. This was personal with Ives, too; Loudon knew. Ives would be remembering yesterday at the Assiniboine, also. But now all three wheeled and headed to the west at a gallop.

"Ives!" Loudon shouted, anger still hot in him. "Come back and fight, damn you!"

Ives looked over his shoulder and shouted something. The three began cutting to the north, toward the river breaks. Loudon cased his gun and knelt down beside the girl and fumbled her shirt open. He saw the soft whiteness of her shoulder and the bright blood. He got his neckerchief off and folded against her wound, holding back the bleeding. The bullet had passed high through her shoulder. He felt relieved, but he felt furious, too, and the odd part was that his anger flared as much against her as against Ives.

"You little fool!" he said. "What were you doing out here alone?"

"Riding," she said. "I went into a coulee. There were cattle held there—Long Nine cattle. Those men saw me. They started chasing me, and shooting."

He helped her to a comfortable sitting position. "Do you think you could ride again?"

She nodded.

He went and caught up both horses. "I'll take you to Craggy Point first. That's nearer than Long Nine. I want that wound fixed up proper."

"I guess I owe you my life," she said. She shut her eyes hard as if to close out all that had happened.

"Come," he said and helped her to a stand.

Queer, he was thinking, how the choice had been made for him. He'd have to go back to the ranch now, at least long enough to deliver her safely, but he reckoned he could stay when he got there. Frome wouldn't be holding it against him for burying Joe McSween, not after his getting Elizabeth Bower out of her fix. It would be Hail the conquering hero! And the truth was just as Ike Nicobar had seen it: a man had to belong to one breed or another. It was follow Frome's way or Ives' way, and he'd just had another sample of Ives' way.

But there was something else mixed into this. Even last night with the dirt freshly shoveled into Joe's grave, he had been reluctant to leave Long Nine. He couldn't fool himself now by pretending he was sorry that he could go back to the ranch. Ambitious, Joe had called him. Could it be that for all his grieving over Joe, what counted most was his own need? Somehow he didn't want to think about that.

7

The Woman

FROME'S MIND HAD TURNED TO THE WOMAN AGAIN. SHE had been on the edge of his thinking for a long while, but sometimes she came crowding, like now, and the question would arise: how much could he risk? He glanced quickly at Grady Jones and Charley Fuller, afraid that his face might show his thoughts. Both were riding along silently, not looking his way. The three had come down from the head of Prickly, and with the afternoon nearly gone, they were picking their way among the potholes of the level country with the Long Nine buildings in sight. Frome looked north. He could be to the river by early dusk.

What would Jones and Fuller think if they knew about the woman and the wondering he was doing, the planning? But hell, he didn't have to account to the likes of them! Still, there were certain qualities by which men were measured in this country, and he wanted to stand high. He had his political ambitions to consider. Cowhands were more apt to be concerned with how a man sat his saddle, for instance, than how he stood on the Territory's vital issues, such as whether the capital should remain at Helena, and what was to be done with the hundreds of Cree Indians who'd fled down from Canada with the close of the Riel Rebellion and were making a mighty nuisance of themselves. No, a man wouldn't get votes in Montana by baby-kissing. And he wouldn't get votes by fooling around with another man's wife. Not if the fact got out. He'd better keep that in mind before he took any step he might be sorry for later.

Charley Fuller spoke up. "It was Jess Loudon buried McSween." Charley was the one who fussed endlessly over a hackamore in the bunkhouse evenings. His small, pinched face was tight with thought. "That shovel came from our blacksmith shop."

The same conclusion had been reached by Frome hours earlier. He had taken these men up into the hills to do a burying job and found the work already done. Frome had made swift deductions. Loudon had been Joe McSween's friend, and Loudon had been missing from the ranch this morning. The Long Nine shovel merely cinched it. Charley was mighty slow in the think department. Frome liked better the other man, Grady Jones, who, a while before, had spied a saddled Texas horse grazing and had laid his loop on the mount and now led the animal along. Joe McSween's horse. Jones hadn't spent half the afternoon figuring out the obvious.

"We should have picked up this broomtail last night," Jones had remarked. "It was mighty dark, though."

A found horse might be found money. Frome had made a mental note to keep an eye on Grady Jones. A Texan, raw-boned and slow of speech and young-old like many of his kind, the man gave promise of being of foreman caliber someday. A ranch got built by having the kind of crew that watched out for its interests in all the ways. Men like Jess Loudon.

Where was Loudon now, and would Long Nine ever see him again? Frome remembered that he'd been dubious about hiring Loudon, wondering at the time if Loudon was of the restless breed that stayed a season and drifted, so he'd put some questions to him. Loudon had been a buffalo hunter, and a few other things before that, probably. Maybe one of those who'd ridden beyond the law and left another name on another range, as some whispered Grady Jones had.

Well, he'd watched Loudon from the first. And with time passing, he'd seen how Loudon stood out, a man willing to do more than was expected of him, a man eager to learn, as though he had his eye on something ahead and was readying himself for it. You didn't find that kind every day. He didn't want to lose Loudon. A man was a tool to the hand, and some came sharp and some came blunt.

Grady Jones said, "Do I smell supper cooking, or is that in my head?"

The ranch buildings lay due east now. And now the woman came back into Frome's mind more strongly than ever. He neck-reined to the north. "I'm going to Latcher's," he said.

"Alone?" Charley Fuller asked and looked scared.

"Alone," Frome said firmly.

"Watch out for the ridges and the coulees," Jones said.

Frome rode his solitary way. He let his gaze rove to the humped hills on the one horizon and the upthrust of the badlands on the other. Distances out here still fooled him some; the air was so much thinner here than in Ohio. A big land this, a promising land. A country that called for leadership that was firm-handed.

What a sight of miles he'd covered when he'd set out a few years back to locate a ranch! He remembered the rim-rock-capped Yellowstone, and the breaks along the Musselshell, and the whole wide face of this lonely eastern Montana world. Not enough water at one place—too far to wood at another. Well, he'd finally found what he wanted, but he'd been scoffed at by some who wondered what the hell possessed a man to settle in the shadow of the badlands. He couldn't have answered them. Maybe the badlands called to something deep in him. Anyhow, he'd made oats grow here, and potatoes; he'd even set out an orchard of apple trees the first spring, though the trees hadn't done very well.

Time enough in the future for a multitude of experiments, but just now he had to establish law and order. The first blow had been struck last night, and high time, too. Civil law and the courts had surely been tried and found wanting, and a man had to do something to protect his investment from thieves. Something drastic.

The Montana Stockgrowers' Association had recognized that fact, but they'd done a lot of shilly-shallying around. At the 1884 meeting quite a lot of members had waved their arms and shouted to raise an army of cowboys and raid the rustler hideouts, which meant just about every abandoned steamboat wood yard, now that the railroad was beginning to drive the boats from the river. Granville Stuart, from over in the Judith country, had spoken against open war, and mighty good news that must have been for Idaho Jack Ives and his ilk. They'd turned bolder. So last summer that same Granville Stuart had headed up posses in his righteous wrath and cleaned out the rustlers in his own section. Slick as a whistle. Earned his outfit the name of Stuart's Stranglers, but they'd got the job done.

And now Long Nine was faced with the same necessity. And by the Lord, the clean-up would come. It had to if this emptiness through which he now rode was ever to be peopled. Meanwhile, though, he'd be going ahead with plans he'd already shaped. On the flats to the south was a line shack not much used any more. He'd have his crew drag it closer to the ranch buildings and make it into a schoolhouse. Elizabeth would do the teaching. The Singletons had three children and the Cottrells one, and there were a couple more at Looped L. A few would be flushed out of the coulees, dusky offspring of wolfers and whiskey peddlers and other careless gentry. Elizabeth would have her hands full.

He frowned, thinking of Elizabeth. Damn it, she was Jonathan Bower with a girl's face. This morning in the kitchen he might have been feeling her father's reproachful stare, the way he had years ago, a stare that said more than any thousand words Jonathan Bower could have flung about that inheritance. At least the inheritance was still in existence, and its name was Long Nine. The girl would own it one day. Surely she wasn't such a ninny as to overlook that and hold against him things past.

". . . I warn you that I'll be watching you," she had said. Let her watch! He had long ago learned that you had to turn one face to the world and keep your real self hidden. Fools never understood that to be a big man you had to be bold. When you got big enough, it was, "Yes, sir, Mr. Frome. Thank you, Mr. Frome," and the how of your growing didn't matter then.

Not much daylight left now. A faint, faraway popping, like the sound of a distant whiplash, caught his attention. He peered this way and that, and then, far to the northeast, he thought he made out riders. Three of them? No, four; one was out ahead. He squinted, trying to see them more clearly. He guessed he should make it a habit to carry field glasses on his saddle. Those riders were firing; that accounted for the popping noise. He could scarcely see them now; they were getting farther away all the time. Cowboys from some upriver ranch, likely, heading for Craggy Point and shooting for the fun of it. The reckless fools!

He rode on. The day faded around him, the earth becoming as smoky as the sky, and in the last light he came to the rim of the river breaks with Latcher's log house below him. As he looked at the house, the thought of the woman was his only thought, but with it his wariness sharpened. What now, he asked himself. Be bold?

He had the earlier visits to remember. What promise had they implied? He and the woman had made small talk, and he had kept his distance. She had interested him, yes, because she might fit into one of his plans; he had once spoken to her about teaching school. Yet there had been something about the way she had looked at him, something about the devices by which she had kept him there talking when Latcher was away, that had brought her back to mind afterwards.

He began riding down the slant. If Latcher were there, he would say he'd come to tell about last night and Joe McSween. Or how the Stockgrowers' had as good as said they'd back whatever move Long Nine made. But now he could see that Latcher's horse was not in the corral, and his pulse quickened.

A wisp of smoke rose from the chimney; that meant Addie was home. He got to the gate and let his horse stand with trailing reins. He walked to the door of the log house and found it open. It was lamplighting time, but the interior was dark. He said into the darkness, his voice softly probing, "Hello—"

Addie's voice came to him, muffled, "Yes—?"

He stepped inside. He made out stove and table and bed. Addie had flung herself across the bed, lying there face down. She turned now, propping herself upon her right elbow, the movement pulling her dress off one shoulder. He realized that her voice was hoarse, as though she'd been crying.

"Are you ill?" he asked.

"Oh, it's you, Mr. Frome." She began sliding from the bed; her dress folded under her with this effort, and she quickly swung to a sitting position on the edge of the bed and tugged at her skirt. "Excuse me," she said. "I guess I've been dozing." She stood up and struck a match and lifted the lamp chimney. "Is there something you want, Mr. Frome?"

"Where's Clem?"

She pushed back her hair from her forehead. Her face looked hot, and her eyes were brighter than he remembered them. "He went riding about an hour ago. We—we had a quarrel."

There was in the words, in the unnecessary explanation, an invitation recognizable to him. But now he knew from what his wariness was made. He grew alarmed. Everything under the sun had its price tag. He remembered suddenly that she had not been interested in his offer of a teaching position. What would she want?

She said quietly, "I know Clem's ways. He'll not be back till morning."

"Tell him I dropped by," he said. "I'll see him later."

She came toward him and paused within arm's length. She smiled at him. "Must you go?"

"Yes," he said firmly. "I must." For he was thinking that perhaps her price tag had a name on it—and that name was Peter Frome.

Someday he would find himself a wife, but she would be as carefully selected as the land he'd chosen for home and the breeding stock he'd put on that graze. She would have to be fit for an even greater post than mistress of Long Nine; she would someday be the governor's wife. Addie Latcher was no such woman as that. But the wildness still flared in him, and with it the certainty that he could step toward her now and find her arms open. He fought against that thought; no need should ever be so great as to blunt wisdom.

He started toward the door, and she said quickly, "It's a long ride back. Let me make coffee for you."

"No," he said. He walked out. He had the dazed feeling of one who had ventured close to the edge of a cutbank and realized the danger in time. He climbed aboard his horse and brought the mount around, not looking back. He told himself he must never stop here again when he knew she was alone. This was his victory—this realization of danger and the resolve to walk wide of it. But at the same moment and in spite of himself, he wondered if he would indeed stay away.

8

Long Nine

IT WAS A GOOD MORNING. THE SMOKE PALL HAD PARTLY lifted, and the sun showed bright over the badlands to the east. Meadow larks spilled their music from the sky, and a breeze roamed the sage. Loudon, riding along with Elizabeth, had only part of his mind on his surroundings, though. Sometimes they left the south-bound wagon road and cut straight overland, the country stretching vast before them, glinting with dew that wet the horses' fetlocks. But always Loudon's thinking was gray with the remembrance of what had happened yesterday.

He gave Elizabeth a sidelong glance, and she smiled at him. She rode well, he observed, and she didn't act as though her shoulder pained her much. Ike Nicobar had fixed her up as good as any sawbones and then recommended a night's sleep, though Elizabeth had been of a mind to head back to Long Nine at once. Frome might be worried, she said. Loudon promised to scare up some loose rider heading south and ask him to carry word, and he'd flushed a Looped L man out of the Assiniboine. Then he'd taken the girl to the makeshift Craggy Point hotel and got a room for her. He'd bedded down in the livery stable loft.

Sleep had come slow, though, for his mind turned to Jack Ives and his anger flared anew. It must have given Ives a hell of a start to have the girl come upon those rustled cattle, and he guessed that in the same fix he would have chased her. The shooting had come out of Ives' fear, too; you didn't make war on women in this country if you had any other choice. But once he, Loudon, had come on the scene, Ives had got more determined than before. Ives wanted him dead. But why? Just because he was Long Nine? Then he remembered Addie Latcher in the back room of the Assiniboine and guessed how his knowing about her might have worried Ives.

Well, he thought now, jerking the reins harder than he meant to, Ives' trail would cross his another day, and yesterday would be squared for. But his anger was only the gray ashes of last night's fire. No use blowing on those ashes now.

He glanced at Elizabeth again. Nothing ruffled about her, even though she'd gone through something to write home about. The more he saw of this girl, the more he liked her. And she liked him, too; there was always the smile when she looked at him. Then he recalled that she was Frome's niece, and all the boldness went out of his thinking. She wasn't for the likes of Jess Loudon. But, damn it, she could be—someday. He was going to grow as tall as Frome, wasn't he? He could come calling on her then. He liked thinking about that; it gave some point to his ambition, making it more than just cattle and land and being looked up to.

He ran his free hand across his cheeks. He'd borrowed a razor in Craggy Point. He was glad for that. It must have given her a second shock, bad as the rustler's bullet, when she'd seen Jess Loudon's whiskered face rearing up out of nowhere.

"Jess," she asked suddenly, "how long have you worked for my uncle?"

"Since roundup time last fall."

"You like working for him?"

"Biggest spread in these parts."

"I'm talking about the man, not the ranch."

"Frome's a good boss."

"He's treated you fairly, always?"

This startled him. "Frome's an honest man," he said. "Anybody will tell you that."

He wondered what she was driving at, but she lapsed into silence again. He remembered Clem Latcher at the Craggy Point landing, speculating on what it would do to a man to appoint himself judge, jury, and executioner. Had Elizabeth maybe already found a different Frome from the one she'd kissed good-bye two years ago? Had she got wondering what made him different, not understanding that Frome had to steel himself for what must be done? He supposed he should straighten out her thinking about that, but he saw that she was peering southward.

"Look!" she cried.

He swung his own gaze that way and saw the rising dust of riders. Jack Ives was close enough to the surface of his mind so that he thought first of the badlanders and stiffened for the fight. He almost shouted at Elizabeth to turn and cut back toward Craggy Point. Then he saw that the man up ahead of the rest was too big in his saddle to be Ives.

"Frome," he said.

Frome, coming up from Long Nine with some of his crew to meet them. Frome, his broad face showing relief as he drew nearer. Couldn't the man ever learn to balance that big hulk of his in the saddle so as to move with the horse?

Long Nine closed the distance and fanned out and pocketed them, a half dozen of the crew swirling to a stop. Frome drew his horse to a stand and said to Elizabeth, "We got the word from that Looped L boy last night. He said you'd be staying in town till today. Thought we'd better ride out and see you safely home." He swung his gaze to Loudon. "I didn't know you'd be coming along, or I wouldn't have fretted."

Loudon said, "I'm still Long Nine."

Whatever moved across Frome's face was no more to be read than Indian rock scratchings. He had a tired look as though he'd tussled with his pillow all night, and Loudon supposed this had come from worry over Elizabeth. Yet he wasn't sure. Couldn't truly tell the feelings of a man whose mustache hid his mouth.

"I'm sorry about McSween, Jess," Frome said. He swung his horse in beside Elizabeth's and said brusquely, "Let's be on our way." His riders bunched behind him, and Loudon found himself stirrup to stirrup with Ollie Scoggins. They rode southward, not hurrying, and Elizabeth was lost to Loudon up ahead.

Scoggins said, finally, "I didn't reckon I'd see you again, Jess."

Loudon said, "Not this way, you mean. Across a gun, maybe. Out in the badlands."

Scoggins looked more stooped than before from whatever load he was carrying. "I'm glad you're back, Jess. So's Frome, I know. Long Nine owes you a heap. After that Looped L hand spilled his story last night, we rode out and moved those cattle back where they belonged. Not a soul there. After his brush with you, Ives must have figured that coulee too hot to be around."

Loudon said sharply, "You mean Frome tended to

those stolen cattle first and came after Elizabeth second?"

"Hell, Jess, the girl was safe in town. Ives might have come back and drifted those cows."

"I suppose," Loudon said.

The sun stood at noon when they came into the ranchyard. They strung out toward the corrals, and one stood empty save for a Texas horse. Loudon looked, and the world narrowed down to that horse. He hadn't thought he'd be hit so hard. He stared at the horse; and all the remembering came back to him, of that horse at a dozen hitchrails, of Joe moving in on the buffalo and Joe riding up the slant from Craggy Point with a last wave of his arm.

In a way he had said his good-bye to Joe yesterday, when he had realized fully after his brush with Ives how Jess Loudon must stand. But this was a separate matter, having nothing to do with the choice he'd made. He felt no anger. He was moved like something jerked by a string. He swung down from his saddle and crossed over to the corral and flung the gate open. He heard Scoggins call, "*Jess*—!" Scoggins was trying to save him from folly, but he was already into the corral.

He waved his hat at Joe's horse and gave a shout. The horse dashed through the gate, head and mane tossing. He galloped away between two of the outbuildings. No man moved to head him off, but Scoggins looked mighty sick. Frome had dismounted and so had Elizabeth; they stood side by side. Frome was a black blur with a white smudge for a face. Loudon came out of the corral and walked toward him.

Frome said in a low and terrible voice, "Now what the hell was the idea of that, Jess?"

"He was nobody's horse but Joe's."

"And no good to McSween. Are you such a fool as to try to run my corral?"

Loudon said, "The hell with that! Wasn't what you took from Joe the other night enough?"

Darkness gathered on Frome's face, and he looked bigger than any bull and about to burst with fury. He took a step forward, his fists clenched. Elizabeth reached out and laid her fingers on his arm.

"What about what he's just brought back to Long Nine?" she asked coldly. "Don't I balance up for what he's let go?"

Frome looked at her, the heat of temper dying in him. He shook his head like a troubled bear. He looked at Loudon again. "I've been drawn too tight lately, Jess. I'd say that you have been, too. No horse is important enough for us to fight over."

Elizabeth looked hard at Loudon and her lips moved, but she didn't speak. Yet he could hear her saying, "Let it be. Let it be." He wanted to smile at her; he wanted to tell her not to worry because everything was all right. He nodded.

Scoggins said, too loudly, "Where the hell is Sam? I could use a bit of grub."

Scoggins slipped down from his horse and handed the reins to one of his men. He headed for the cook-shack. There was a flurry of movement toward the corrals, and then the others drifted one by one after Scoggins. Frome turned toward the house, taking Elizabeth's arm.

Loudon put his own horse away, then crossed over to the bench beside the cook-shack door and gave his face a splash at the basin there. He used the towel and rubbed the lint from his face with the heels of his hands. He felt as though he'd just come out of a slugging match. He walked inside to find the crew at the long table eating. He closed the door and put his back to it and built up a cigarette. There was something he had to say but first he wanted the right words. He got the smoke fired.

"Listen," he said then. Their heads came up. "One of you tied his hands behind him and put a rope around his neck. I know that. One of you belted his horse out from under him."

Damned if he couldn't hear his own heart beat in the silence that came down when the knives and forks stopped clattering. A chair leg scraped against the planking. He saw a blur of faces that all seemed dead. Only Grady Jones looked square at him, his lips tight and his eyes glinting.

"It was part of your day's work," Loudon went on. "Point is, I never want to know which of you did the last of it. That's all. I just never want to hear about it. That way there'll be no one or two of you I'll have to hate."

He'd got it said. He moved to an empty chair and seated himself. Sam stood sober faced in the doorway between kitchen and mess hall. Loudon's cigarette had gone dead. He fumbled at his pockets for another match, and someone handed him one. He fired the smoke and took two hard drags at it, then stubbed it out in his saucer.

"Pass some grub along, will you," he said and had a platter of steaks thrust at him. The din of knives and forks rose again. He had come home.

To a glum meal, though. The crew was edgy, but it wasn't he who'd made them edgy; he was sure of that. He'd had his say and they'd understood him, and that was the end of it. They weren't holding it against him for turning Joe's horse loose, either; that had been a matter between him and Frome, and no lost face for either of them.

Charley Fuller looked across the table at Loudon.

"That Looped L ranny told it scary last night, but did he tell it true, Jess? The girl got shot by Ives or one of those two with him?"

"She didn't shoot herself," Loudon said.

"Those badlanders must 'a' figgered just to kick up some dust behind her," someone said. "Hitting her was an accident. Frome will figure it that way, won't he?"

"Was she bad hurt, Jess?"

"Grady, you was with the bunch that headed out last night to move those cattle back. Did Frome seem mighty peeved about the girl being hurt?"

"Hell, boys, Frome ain't the kind to let himself be stampeded. He ain't gonna hit the badlanders till he's good and ready."

"That's your notion, Lew. I want to hear what Grady says."

Loudon understood then, hearing the fear behind all their talk. He supposed that fear had been with them a long time, just as it had been with Scoggins, though not showing so plainly on some as it had on the foreman. He caught himself looking over his shoulder at the door, and after a while he heard it open. Even before he read the faces across the table from him, he knew that Frome had entered and that here was the end to waiting. He turned in his chair till he could see Frome.

Frome looked sad and troubled and something else besides. "I've just had a talk with my niece," he said. "Now I have all the details of what happened yesterday. She came upon rustlers. She was chased and fired upon. Deliberately. And she was hit. She wasn't wounded seriously, but that isn't the point. The point is that we've put up with all we can stand."

Scoggins said, "You mean the time has come for the clean-up?"

"How else will it ever be safe for anybody from Long Nine to ride alone?"

"You want us to head out? Right now?"

"What would we gain by waiting?"

"Nothing," Scoggins said. "Which way do we head?"

"I wanted your ideas on that, Ollie."

Scoggins looked about him. His eyes got to Loudon, and this was like the other night in the bunkhouse when Scoggins had asked, "How would you do it, Jess?"

Loudon said, "You can hang around Craggy Point for days, hoping they'll ride in. But they'll have their ears to the ground and know what you're up to. You can scout Prickly, thinking they'll come after more horses, but they'll be hitting somewhere else. If I wanted badlanders, I'd go into the badlands."

Frome said, "You know that country better than the rest of us. Will you lead the way?"

Frome still looked sad and troubled, but now Loudon recognized that other thing in his face. Anger, terrible in its quietness. Anger because of Elizabeth and her hurt? Or because of something else, like his turning Joe's horse loose? But Frome had asked a question: Long Nine had spoken to Long Nine. That was the thing to be considered, no matter what edge of doubt he might have.

"Yes," Loudon said. "I'll lead the way."

9

The Wild Dark

THEY GOT READY TO RIDE AT ONCE. THE CREW GATHERED up guns and packed grub enough for a night and a day, while Frome moved everywhere, giving orders and doing the thinking for those who might have been slipshod about this or that. Frome had a knack for generaling, Loudon reflected. Maybe that was part of what made Frome as big as he was. Take himself, he'd rather do a chore than put someone else at it. Saved a lot of bickering. But he guessed that here was another lesson he could learn from Frome. The big men worked their minds and saved their muscles.

Frome's voice reached across the yard. "Will we need water bags on this ride, Jess?"

"A few for the afternoon. We'll be heading toward the river."

Frome had put on a pair of leather chaps, but he still wore his black broadcloth coat and vest, with the watch chain stretched across it. Frome had buckled on a gun. Inside an hour he had all the crew up in saddles except Sam and a couple of older hands he'd ordered to stay behind to keep an eye on the place. When Long Nine was bunched in the yard, he waved to Loudon to lead off.

They were moving past the ranch-house when Elizabeth came out. She had drawn a shawl around her shoulders and she held it tightly clasped. She stood directly in the way of the riders, and Loudon pulled up, and Frome came stirrup to stirrup with him and looked down at her. She said, "You're going after them, aren't you?"

Frome said, "My dear, we're left with no choice."

"Because of what happened to me yesterday?"

"You might say so."

"Then you go against my will," she said. "Let me make that clear. I told you in the house that more blood spilled won't do any good. I'll not be the excuse for your doing what you so plainly want to do anyway!"

Loudon could see them both: Elizabeth, her hair moving to the breeze, her face severe; Frome, his brows drawn together, his shoulders bunching. If anger rode the man, he was keeping a tight rein on it. He said in the tone of a patient parent with a wilful child, "There are things out here you simply don't understand, Elizabeth. This is one of them. You must not make it personal in your mind. Now go inside, please."

She said, "I couldn't hope to stop you. But I want you to know that I'm not fooled."

She turned then, and Loudon thought that Frome was going to call after her. He almost did so himself. What made this mistrust in her of Frome, and why couldn't she see that Frome really had no choice? Couldn't she remember the warning Jess Loudon had given her on the boat? He felt sorry for Frome and proud of the way Frome kept hold of himself before his men. She had made a hard job harder for Frome.

"Let's ride," Frome said. He shook his head sadly. Loudon gigged his horse and rode out with Long Nine at his back, Frome and Ollie Scoggins and Grady Jones and Charley Fuller and a dozen others.

Frome again moved up till he was beside Loudon. Scoggins came to flank Loudon on the other side, riding half a horse behind. Scoggins' face had a troubled look.

Loudon said, "It won't be a long ride, Ollie."

He led them in a general northeasterly direction, not pushing hard, but fixing the pace to bring him where he wanted to be by sundown. Nice to see the sun again, and maybe that was a good omen, but it struck him that the same sun shone on the badlanders. Good luck was all too often somebody else's bad luck. He crossed from one hogback ridge to another, dropping down into coulees thick with chokeberry bushes and finding places that looked level but were marred by sunken spots. Again he thought of how it was that the badlands merged with the better country so there was no beginning or end to either.

Sometimes he led Long Nine high and could look down upon an expanse of valleys and hills and rolling prairie, but more often they were in the coulee bottoms and had to single file along in a hushed, shut-in world. The men got to tipping the water bags often. All the creeks hereabouts headed up in the badlands and were reddish of water and thick with gumbo.

When the men were able to bunch up, the crew rode around him so silent and glum that he was reminded of a funeral on a rainy day. He knew what was bothering them. They could talk about carrying a war to the badlanders and go through all the motions of getting ready for that war, but it made a man uneasy to think about the real shooting. Not for what he was going to do to whomever he went up against, but what he was going to do to himself.

Then, with the afternoon nearly gone and the depths turned gloomy because the sun couldn't reach here, they were into the badlands for sure. No betwixt and between country this. Weird rock here. Sandstone carved by wind and rain across the silent centuries into shapes like church spires and saddles and kneeling women, and shapes, too, like something out of a bad dream, queer shapes with no sense to them. Color, too, wild and riotous higher up where the sunlight touched. An ancient, magnificent desolation, echoing, likely, the tramp of explorers' feet and holding, along the river, the crumbled leavings of history —trading posts and forts and boat landings. Blackbirds rose in clouds from their nests on high pinnacles. A few bushes grew bravely.

Loudon was leading Long Nine toward the river. As he drew close to it, he called a halt, and here they wrapped the hooves of their horses with sacking they'd fetched along. After that they mounted again and were ghost men riding in a ghost world.

A half hour of this and Frome asked, "Just where are you leading us?"

"To the old Castle Bend wood yard," Loudon said.

This choice came from a hunch he was playing, thanks to a random remark Joe McSween had dropped when they'd met on the prairie a month ago and stopped to smoke and pass the time of day. Joe had been lined up with Jack Ives even then, and making no bones about it. He'd mentioned the wood yard, and the remark had stuck with Loudon, though now it seemed a little like cheating, this using what Joe had said to bring a war to Joe's saddle-mates. But if you looked at it as a war, then everything was fair.

Shortly he drew rein and lifted a hand. "Better stop here."

They had been following another of those narrow ravines. They dismounted and stood in little groups, keeping close to each other and not talking loud. Loudon knew that what held them hushed was that same smell of trouble that made Ollie Scoggins look so worried. Here was what they had feared at the noon meal when Elizabeth had come home with blood spilled. Here was the clean-up. It wasn't cowardice that quieted them down. He knew that, for their feelings were his own, and understandable.

He drew out his six-shooter and looked at it. The gun was a tool of his trade, but nobody here was itching to use one against another man. He moved away from the men and climbed a side of the ravine to a ridge and bellied down atop it. He could see quite a sweep of country. Below, the river wound, sluggish and muddy; and across the river the cliffs rose nearly straight up from the water, white sandstone looking like an ancient fortress with towers and windows agleam in the last light.

Nearer, on this side of the river, was a stretch of openness in which stood an old abandoned wood yard that had once supplied fuel for the steamers when the river traffic was thicker. Most of the larger willows and cottonwoods along the Missouri at this point were gone, but a few still stood among high brush. Near the bank was a log cabin and a stable and a large corral, all in fair repair. Plenty of horses in that corral. A wisp of smoke rose from the cabin's mud chimney. The old stockade that had once protected the woodhawks from Indians had largely fallen into ruin.

A man showed at the doorway of the cabin, and Loudon tried to lie flatter. The man walked half a hundred paces to the Missouri, a bucket in his hand. He filled the bucket and came back to the cabin. Two other men loomed in the doorway, awaiting him. Voices lifted, far away and meaningless. The three vanished into the cabin.

Loudon heard a wheezing breath and saw Frome climbing up beside him. He made a flat gesture with his hand, urging Frome to keep his head down. Frome got closer and had his look, too, squinting hard. Loudon wondered how Frome felt with the fight so near.

Frome asked in a whisper, "How many down there?"

"Three have showed," Loudon said. "Must be more. Quite a bunch of horses. Some are mounts for the men; the rest are stolen stock, I'd guess. You'll find your Prickly cayuses down there."

Frome grunted. "How do we handle this?"

"It's almost dark enough. We divide up and move in on them. Send some men with Ollie and have them follow the coulee to the river and ease along the bank to cut off the cabin bunch if they make a run that way. Some others can flank the place to the south. The rest of us go over this ridge and straight at the cabin."

Frome grunted again and began sliding down the slope. Loudon followed him. The sun was gone behind western ridges, and darkness was creeping into the badlands. Frome's voice made a low rumble as he moved among the men. Loudon recognized Scoggins' tall, bent form and saw Scoggins walk off, three of the crew with him. Grady Jones led another batch along the ravine in the opposite direction.

Frome and four others still stood. Charley Fuller's voice came huskily: "Now?"

"No," Loudon said. "We wait. Ollie and the others have more ground to cover."

He stood in the growing night, trying to keep his mind empty, trying not to think about the other side of that ridge. He recalled the morning and his ride from Craggy Point with Elizabeth; the morning seemed far removed. He waited. He could hear the river; he could hear the beat of an axe over yonder as someone toiled outside the cabin, cutting wood for a supper fire, likely. He supposed he should be hungry, but he wasn't.

After a while he raised his hand, then turned and began to climb the ridge again.

Frome was right behind him when he reached the top, the others straggling along. Hard now to make out detail below, but the cabin had a rectangle of light at a window facing this way, and Loudon marked that light and started down the slope toward it. Now the job had been reduced to this simple thing: keep in line with the cabin; keep moving.

He heard Frome lumber along after him; he heard the roll of pebbles as others came. *Loud! Too loud!* He expected to see a stir from the cabin, but the darkness stayed unbroken below. He wondered where Ollie Scoggins walked, and Grady Jones. He got down the far side of the ridge and waited while the men grouped behind him. Frome was at his elbow; he sensed that Frome was full of questions he didn't dare ask for fear even a whisper might carry. Loudon walked directly toward the cabin and heard Frome fall into step beside him. No shortage of courage in Frome, Loudon thought; no shoving others ahead of him. And then somebody said out of the darkness before the cabin, "Who's there?"

Loudon stopped. He held down his hand in that flat

gesture meant to stay the others, hoping those behind him could see it.

"Who's there?" the voice demanded again, uncertainty giving the question a sharper edge. "Damn it, speak up!"

Someone cut loose with a gun, some nervous one like Charley Fuller. It was a wild shot, aimed at nothing. Instantly the light went out in the cabin. The man who'd challenged Long Nine lifted a yell and went running, the beat of his boots seeming to be everywhere and nowhere. Loudon lunged after him. All around, guns sounded—that was Long Nine caught up in the madness that had loosed the first shot. The cliff across the river hurled back the echoes.

Loudon shouted, "Look where you're shooting, you damn' fools!"

Men made heavier shadows against the cabin wall; men were spilling out of the cabin and running toward the river. One of them was shouting, and Loudon knew that voice to be Jack Ives'. His anger of yesterday came back then; and for the first time, this day's doings became personal to him. He lifted his own gun and fired in the direction of the voice.

Six or seven badlanders here, he guessed. Certainly not the full bunch. No counting them for sure; they were only shadows with legs under them. Long Nine pounded hard after them, and from the direction of the river gunfire arose. That would be Ollie Scoggins' bunch trying to cut them off. Grady Jones and his crew were the only ones not in the hot part, the way things had broken.

Loudon shouted, "Ollie—?" He listened hard over the rattle of gunfire for an answer. Did Ollie reply, or was that the cliff giving back the echo of his own voice? He thought he heard Jones' men coming up. He called, "Some of you string around that corral and keep them from their horses." Just then someone shouted from the river, "They've got a boat!"

Men shaped up out of the south, and Grady Jones called Frome's name. Jones came up with others at his back. He asked, "What the hell's going on?"

Frome said, "We've botched it. They've got away, I think."

Someone cried, "Long Nine!" to identify himself and took shape out of the night. This was Tex Corbin, an older hand, who'd been with Scoggins. He was almost weeping with anger. "They had a skiff," he reported. "We made it hot for them as they shoved off. We may have nicked one. It was Jack Ives' bunch, all right."

"Might as well get a light burning," Loudon said. On the river bank guns still banged, but they didn't seem to have any spirit behind them. Loudon's mouth tasted cottony.

He groped his way into the cabin and found a lantern, the chimney still hot to the touch. He got the lantern burning. Nothing much in this cabin but a stove and a table and chairs and a scattering of clothes and riding gear. From such a rendezvous as this, stock was shoved across the river and whiskey was peddled to the Indians; the smell of bedbugs was here. Frome came in and looked around. His ponderous features might have been stone.

Grady Jones came in shortly. "You should see what we found in the stable. A stack of fresh hides folded and salted and ready for shipping down river. Looped L and Boxed C and Long Nine and Singleton's Rafter S among the brands. Those horses in the corral came from just about every spread hereabouts, too, not to mention a few brands I never heard of before." His face was tight with anger. "This nest needed cleaning out long ago."

"We'll take the horses back to the ranch," Frome said. He looked at Loudon. "You did a good job of finding the right place and getting us to it, Jess. Whatever was done right tonight was because of your planning." He looked toward the doorway. "Where's Ollie?"

Grady Jones carried the question to the door and flung it out to the waiting men. Ollie's name moved among them like a ball tossed aimlessly.

Frome picked up the lantern and said, "Let's go looking."

Loudon knew then. He knew in his bones, because there had been something about Ollie today that had showed the foreman knew, too, just as a steer knows when a bad storm is coming. Why else hadn't Ollie rejoined them?

Loudon went with the others, Frome leading them, with the lantern swinging in his hand and his shadow big and clumsy. The river lay like black silver under the sky, and they searched among the rocks along the bank until they found what they sought. After that they were as silent as an empty church. Loudon saw what the lantern showed and then looked up at the cliff across the river. No castle now, that cliff, but a hugeness of weight poised above them, black and forbidding.

Some dead ones, Loudon thought, look as though they're asleep; but Ollie Scoggins looked dead, and he was, his mouth slack and his eyes staring. A stray shot fired by Ives' bunch as they had fought their way to the skiff had done this to Ollie.

Charley Fuller said, "Looks like this outfit needs itself a new foreman," making it cocky to hide something that lay deep in him. Then his voice broke, and he said, "God damn them!" He kept saying it over and over.

Someone said, "We couldn't see the skiff because of that old cottonwood up the bank. We didn't know they had any boat."

Frome looked calm, and Loudon wondered if the man really felt nothing or if by showing steadiness he hoped to steady them all. Frome said, "We'd better bring our horses over the ridge and camp here till daylight. Nothing more we can do tonight." He gestured with the lantern. "A couple of you carry Ollie out of here."

So it was. Afterwards there was the night with men blanket-wrapped in and out of the cabin, and some standing guard along the river bank against the small chance that Ives would be foolish enough to venture back. Starlight tonight, and the river clamorous and the badlands all around, and somewhere, distantly, a coyote sounding lonely as God.

Sleeplessness tonight, with men turning in their blankets, and Loudon staring into the sky and remembering Ollie—remembering especially how Ollie had come to him in the bunkhouse, needing him because the job ahead was too big. Well, the wind had tipped over the pine tree . . .

He saw the day come and watched the camp break up. He saw the blanket-wrapped body athwart Ollie's saddle, and men spilling the horses out of the corral and bunching them. He got astride his own horse and made ready to fall in with the others. Yesterday he had done the leading, but nobody needed the trail home pointed out. He wondered if Frome would think to touch a match to cabin and stable; but when Frome didn't, he offered no advice.

Frome came to him just as they lined out, jogging

his horse toward Loudon's. Frome had a black shadow of beard, and his eyes were tired. He said, "When we get back, you can move your stuff from the bunkhouse, Jess. You're foreman now."

"Sure," Loudon said and supposed he should be glad. Here was a next step taken, and what was the good in counting the cost when it was already paid? Why the hell did he always have that edge of doubt? He guessed he was tired and that was why his only real feeling was emptiness.

10

Gathering Storm

FOREMAN . . .

It was, Loudon came to think, an experience to make a man proud. Foreman of Long Nine, with nearly twenty men to take his orders. Foreman, with a room to himself in the big house, and Frome talking affairs with him each morning and respecting his judgment, counting on him. And Elizabeth at the breakfast table, too, though not often, for with the school established and her doing the teaching, she usually stayed at the schoolhouse overnight, the light from her window shining across the prairie . . .

It kept a man busy, being foreman. It seemed to Loudon that his days had got fuller than he'd ever supposed they could be. It was take a couple of boys and fix that line fence, Grady; and you, Bill or Pete or Lennie, head up Prickly and have a look at those horses. Here's a waterhole that needs to be dug out, and there's gear to be overhauled for the fall roundup. October's coming, and we've got a herd of cattle soon into Miles. A time for breaking horses now. Thunder in the corrals and a big stir everywhere. Get up at the crack of dawn and ride and work and worry through all the long day. Remember that you can't do everything yourself, that you've got to learn to pass out the chores to the others. Make your reports to Frome and hope they find his favor, for he's picked you out from the rest of the crew. And some like Grady Jones have been scowling about it, figuring they'd been on the payroll longer. Grady was looking mighty sour these days.

Yes, it made a man proud, being foreman. Gone was the first irony of thinking how Ollie Scoggins had had to die before the job could be Loudon's. A man shouldn't quarrel with the good things that luck threw his way. And when ranch affairs took him to Craggy Point in the weeks following the ruckus at Castle Bend, Ike Nicobar was beaming proud of him. It did Loudon good, seeing Ike so happy over what had happened to an old friend and partner.

No sign of Jack Ives since that night when the man had fought his way to the river bank and left Ollie Scoggins dead in the rocks. Just the same, Loudon rode warily. No stir of trouble around Long Nine, though Looped L and Boxed C and Rafter S had all reported losing stock.

Singleton of Rafter S had paid a visit to Long Nine one day. He'd crooked a leg around his saddle-horn and fingered his skimpy goatee and said, "I'll make my business short, Frome. How about your outfit joining up with mine in a real clean-up? No half-cocked deal like you pulled at Castle Bend."

Frome had stood on his front porch, Loudon at his elbow. Frome said, "When the time comes, Shad."

Singleton spat into the dust. "You've swapped even with them," he said. "A man for a man—McSween for Scoggins. Maybe you aim to quit with the books balanced. You'll find out you can't. More blood will be spilled. If we're wise, we'll spill it first."

Singleton was a Texan. Loudon knew the breed, for he'd been born to it; hundreds like Singleton had never surrendered in their hearts at Appomattox. They had followed Chisholm's dust and Goodnight's to far ranges when the Texas plains had been overgrazed after the war. They had seen their bearded reflections in the Bosque Grande and the Cimarron and the Yellowstone, and they were a fighting breed long used to hitting first if they were to hit at all.

But Frome shook his head. "I'll hit when I'm ready, Shad. And not before. You spoke about a half-cocked job at Castle Bend. I'll do it right next time."

Singleton dropped his boot to the stirrup. "Someday a Rafter S man will get winged by a badlander. That day I'll be riding to war. And I'll be counting on you and the others to back me, whether you figure you're ready or not."

Frome, it seemed to Loudon, had got like Ollie Scoggins had been, a man whose mind was always on something else. Maybe what had happened to Scoggins had taught Frome that war was a blade that cut two ways. Still, Frome's mouth set harder than it had before, and he had made it plain to Singleton that Long Nine would strike again. Frome would pass Scoggins' grave without a sideward glance—they'd buried Ollie on a little rise near the ranch-house—but it was plain to see that Frome hadn't forgotten.

The first days after the raid he'd had the stolen horses they'd recovered cut out brand by brand, and he'd given Loudon the job of seeing that those belonging to Long Nine's neighbors were returned. But others were from distant ranches, and a few were military horses from the far-flung forts, and a couple of the brands were Canadian. Those horses were out on Long Nine graze now. Loudon had pointed out that if word were sent to the owners, they could at least come after their stock. Frome had nodded, but as far as Loudon knew, he'd made no move as yet to get shed of the horses.

Elizabeth had spoken of the matter to Frome one morning at breakfast, but still the chore wasn't done.

Elizabeth was busy these days, too, busy as Loudon. Long Nine had snaked up that line shack and got it rigged with benches for the children and a makeshift desk for her. There was a stove in the place and a table, and there was a bed in a lean-to so that Elizabeth could stay the night any time she felt it best not to make the ride of three or four miles back to the ranch-house. Frome had at first protested her overnight absences, thinking, likely, of Jack Ives and the badlanders. But with the days passing peacefully, Elizabeth took more and more to staying at the schoolhouse. Loudon, riding past the place by day, would listen to the hum of voices or find a queer delight in seeing three or four children skylined aboard some old pensioner of a saddle horse as they headed homewards. Nights when Elizabeth didn't show at the ranch, Loudon sometimes rode out to where he could see her light burning.

On one such night, he came back to the corral to find Tex Corbin awaiting him. "Frome wants to see you," Corbin said.

His horse put up, Loudon walked to the house and into the big parlor and found Frome before the fireplace, where Scoggins had stood the night Elizabeth had first come back to Long Nine. Damned if the remembrance of that night wasn't so strong in Loudon that he could smell the coffee they'd drunk.

Frome had built a small fire; the evenings were cool now. He faced about, smiling. "All going well, Jess?"

Loudon nodded.

"Sit down," Frome invited and waved him toward one of the chairs, but Loudon chose to stand. Frome fingered his watch chain and then said, "I had my eye on Grady Jones as a possible foreman, if the need ever arose. Perhaps that was plain to the crew. And perhaps you've wondered why I chose you instead."

Loudon shrugged. "You've had the badlanders on your mind for a long time. I was never one of them, but I had a friend who was. That's how I guessed what we'd find at the wood yard. Maybe you were thinking that the things I knew would help."

Frome nodded. "That's partly true. We've still got a clean-up to make, but not at the decision of that fire-eating fool Singleton. But about the foremanship, I was looking far beyond that. You want to amount to something, Jess. Jones would look after himself first, Long Nine second. Right?"

"Grady makes a good hand."

"And you make a good foreman. I think we're going to get along, Jess."

Again Loudon shrugged. In the nights, he'd turned over in his mind the question as to why Frome had chosen him, not truly knowing the answer; he did not know it now. Once he'd stood up against Frome—that day he turned Joe McSween's horse loose—and he'd never been quite sure that Frome had forgiven him. Yet shortly after that, Frome had made him foreman. Could the man be afraid of him? Had Frome been the wise man who'd turned an enemy into an ally and so disarmed him? He didn't know, and he didn't like this small talk that seemed to get nowhere. "Was this what you wanted to see me about?" he asked.

"No," Frome said. "As a matter of fact, word's come that we've got a herd waiting at the Miles City bedding grounds. The trail boss asks me to send half a dozen of my crew to pick up the cattle. Most of the trail crew will head back south, though a few want to stay in Montana and will come on to the Missouri. You can pick your Long Nine men, Jess. Better take one who can cook and one who'll be good at wrangling horses."

Loudon said, "Grady will be fine. Tex Corbin, too, and Pete Wickes. Lennie Hastings and Paul Grant."

"I'd rather Grady stayed here," Frome said. "He'll make a good strawboss while you're gone." He was thoughtful for a moment. "I'll tell you what. Ride over to Latcher's tomorrow and get Clem to go to Miles with you. That will make one less hand off Long Nine."

"Sure," Loudon said.

Next morning he passed the schoolhouse as he headed for Latcher's. He rode near enough to hear the children's voices lifted in song, but he didn't stop. He reached Latcher's after noon and told Clem the wishes of Frome and got Clem's agreement to make an extra hand. Latcher promised to be at Long Nine early tomorrow. Loudon had a bite to eat, Addie serving him but not saying much. He was glad to get out of Latcher's and go riding up the slope.

Funny how even the land looked different since he'd become foreman. He saw it now as graze to stock the cattle that were bedded at Miles, those critters and other herds to come. A cow on grass was more than something to please the eye; it was a mark in the ledgers Frome kept; it was a promise for the future. The glimmering white of buffalo bones made a man like Ike Nicobar sad, but the wise man looked ahead, not behind . . .

Rain came on the homeward ride, a spatter of drops at first, hissing in the dust, and then a downpour that had Loudon unfastening his slicker from behind his saddle. He rode into the early dusk that the storm brought, heading always southward and letting his horse find its way. Thunder came, and lightning that flushed the world in a chalky glare. A good hard rain this, cold enough for late autumn.

Rain still pelted down when he sighted the light of the schoolhouse, and he rode that way and dismounted. Long Nine had put up a shed for Elizabeth's horse, and there was room in it for his own. He groped to the schoolhouse. Thunder boomed as he pounded the door, but he thought he heard Elizabeth cry, "Who's there?" He'd insisted that she keep a gun with her, and he was mindful of this as he shouted his name. The door opened, and he lurched inside. He took off his slicker and flung it across one of the benches. He removed his hat and let the rain run from its brim to a puddle about his feet.

He grinned at Elizabeth. "Some night!"

The lamp was on her desk in a far corner. Lightning came, making the room so livid that everything stood out starkly—benches and desk and stove—and then the thunder roared, and the lamp's flame shook.

Elizabeth said in a tight voice, "I'm glad you came. I'm afraid of thunder and lightning when I'm alone. Isn't that silly?"

"I reckon not. Me, I'm afraid of any kind of a snake, even a dead one." He moved toward the stove and held his hands out to it; she came up and joined him. "How's your shoulder?" he asked.

"Still a bit sore."

He looked about. "I didn't think you'd stay here, a night like this."

"I kept waiting," she said, "hoping it would let up a little."

"Frome should have sent someone after you."

"No," she said. "He knows I wouldn't want any

special consideration like that. Besides, I'd rather be here."

Something in her voice aroused his curiosity more than her words did. He knew that some kind of barrier stood between her and Frome. At those breakfast sessions they were both mighty polite to each other, but still they were like two people with drawn guns. He wondered if the tight feeling between them had got started the day of Castle Bend, when Elizabeth had stood in the yard and accused Frome before all his crew of using her wound as an excuse for a badlander clean-up. Was Elizabeth now remembering Ollie Scoggins beneath a mound of dirt? Or had the wall between her and Frome been reared long before that? He remembered thinking in Craggy Point, the day he'd sat with Ike talking about Joe McSween, that the girl had worries of her own that were maybe built around Frome.

He searched her face. "Frome's a good man."

"Is he?" She seated herself on a bench and cupped her chin in her hands and stared at the stove. Fire danced around the edge of the lids.

Loudon sat down beside her. He asked bluntly, "What is it that's eating at you?"

"Those horses he's still holding. Has he notified the owners yet?"

"I don't think so."

"Then isn't that the same as stealing them?"

He turned this over in his mind. "If you look at it that way. This is a big country, so big that things get done slow compared to the way they're done where you come from. Frome's job is to think of Long Nine. Everything else has to come second. Someday he'll find the time to send me or one of the boys to notify those ranchers."

"I wonder," she said.

She looked tired, and he guessed this teaching job was harder than anyone supposed. Riding herd on a bunch of kids could be tough. Rain sounded on the roof; the steady drumming together with the heat of the stove turned him drowsy, and he was content just to sit, saying nothing. He wondered why it calmed him merely to be near her, yet he had a sense of disappointment, too. He remembered how she'd looked aboard the *Prairie Belle,* so quick and graceful, but with a roguishness that had made him think she could kick up her heels if she liked. He'd hoped that with knowing her better, he'd see more of her livelier side. Instead, she'd turned glummer with each week on Long Nine. It made him feel cheated.

She said softly, dreamily, "Raining tonight. Raining all over the world."

Then the lightning came again, throwing its chalky glare into the far corners, and the darkness tromped hard after it, the thunder booming. He felt her arms go around him frantically, and he held her tight against him. Without intending to, he hunted for her lips with his own, being gentle about this. His lips brushed her cheek. She pushed at him, her hands against his chest. He ceased trying to kiss her, but he still held her. She sighed.

He said, "If ever anything troubles you and I can help, send for me."

"No," she said. "Once I thought I could do that. But he's bought you since, by giving you the foremanship."

He shook his head. "That doesn't make a lick of sense."

"Only because you don't know him as well as you think you do."

A lot of people had their own particular crazy streak, and he guessed this was hers—this distrust of

Frome's every move. He'd known a man once who was as even keeled as anybody until he got on the subject of religion. Spent all his time painting Scripture verses on rocks, while his wife and children went hungry. He thought of this man while he held Elizabeth in the gloom.

Finally he realized the rain was slackening. He loosed her gently and stood up. "I've got to be going," he said. "I hit the trail early tomorrow for Miles." He felt awkward. "What I said about helping you still goes."

She stood up, too. She looked unhappy, and he wanted to comfort her, but he'd made one try and failed. No getting around her feeling about Frome. But, damn it, there couldn't be anything solid behind her distrust! He waited for her to speak, but she said nothing, and he turned toward the door. He picked up his slicker and hat and donned these. "Goodnight," he said. And he rode away with the feeling that he'd come closer to her tonight than ever before, yet that somehow they now stood farther apart than after he'd kissed her so roughly aboard the *Prairie Belle.*

11

On The Trail

THIS HAD BEEN A DAY OF SAGE, ENDLESS MILES OF SAGE, sweet smelling after last night's rain; and the six who'd ridden across it had made noon camp on Box Elder Creek and put the Musselshell behind them in early afternoon. Now, at campfire time, Loudon heard the sizzle of bacon in a frying pan and smelled the good smell of coffee and felt tired and satisfied. A clear sky tonight, and the smoke of the campfire pointed straight upward. Good weather in the making, and with luck they'd camp on Sunday Creek tomorrow night. The morning after that they should be in Miles City taking delivery of that Texas herd.

Everything was going as well as Loudon could have hoped. True, there'd been the business of this morning when they'd come upon a bunch of Cree who'd begged food and tobacco, but there'd been no real trouble then or since. A ragged bunch of redskins, those, and hungry looking, too, Loudon recalled, fugitives from the Queen's justice since the collapse of the Rebellion up in Saskatchewan last spring. But those

Cree today hadn't looked much like revolutionists but only like people who hadn't been eating often lately. Four or five bucks and some squaws and papooses, and only one rifle showing among them.

Loudon's crew was traveling light. They'd get meat from antelopes they might knock over with their guns, but they were packing bacon and had a good supply of tobacco. Trouble was, all Indians were a thorn in the side of the stockmen, and these were connected by blood and tribal ties to Montana's own Blackfeet, Bloods and Gros Ventres, and so roamed far and wide. Range cattle fed them, and horse-stealing gave them their fun; and any appeal by the ranchers to the military got so tangled up in petitions that folks itched to take up Winchesters and settle the business in their own fashion.

No, it hadn't pleased Loudon to run into those pesky redskins, and an Indian was an Indian and so of not much account, whether he was a fugitive from Canada or a young buck off a Montana reservation. But there'd been something about the blank-faced squaws and the unblinking, shoe-button-eyed papooses in this morning's bunch that had moved Loudon. Damn it, when a man's own belly was tight from good feeding, it was hard to be blind to the hunger in another's face! Still, it was Long Nine's grub he was toting, and so he'd hesitated. And while he'd been trying to make up his mind, Tex Corbin said, "Frome ain't going to be wanting us to feed these beggars."

Corbin was a Texas man, with a Texan's memory of Comanche deviltry. This was Loudon's heritage, too; but in him was a sharper, nearer remembrance, that of Elizabeth in the schoolhouse last night being doubtful of Frome. And so Corbin's remark struck him wrong.

"The hell with Frome," Loudon had said. "We can spare a little bacon and a few plugs of Climax."

Seemed that Tex wasn't holding that against him this evening, and Tex wasn't likely to run to Frome on their return and tell him how his soft-hearted foreman had been kind to a bunch of stinking, thieving Indians. Tex wasn't cut to that pattern. A sorehead like Grady Jones maybe, but not Tex. Right now Tex was forking bacon to tin plates, and the others, crowding close, were joshing him. All except Clem Latcher.

Damned if Latcher wasn't out of place in this bunch. No wildness in him, no rioting joy of living as in Tex Corbin and Pete Wickes and Lennie Hastings and Paul Grant. The last three were young and feeling their oats, but it wasn't the years that made the difference, for they were akin to Tex Corbin, yes, and to Jess Loudon, too, by being frontier born. No soft faces there, and eyes like a dog's that had been left out in the rain. Trouble with Clem was that he was colorless inside and out, just a long, gangling drink of water who'd read too many books. And tried to live with a woman too hot-blooded for him. A good enough hand on the trail, Clem, never quibbling about whether it was his turn to fetch a bucket of water or take a look at the horses. But there was no solid bottom to him, no real oak.

Hell, Loudon thought, *this man is my friend;* and he was ashamed of such shabby notions as he'd just had about Clem. Yet how could he truly be friend to a man he pitied? Could anybody cotton to someone they felt sorry for, since feeling sorry took away respect? Yet he respected Clem for his book learning. Yes, and for the little courtesies of the man. Come to think about it, just because he'd wintered with Clem, he used some words in his mind that you didn't hear around a bunkhouse.

Supper eaten, the men spun up cigarettes and stretched themselves by the fire. Someone wanted to know about the herd they'd be fetching home.

"Three thousand head of Texas cattle," Loudon said. "Frome told me this morning. A dry herd. The cow and calf herd is a month back on the trail."

Pete Wickes said, "Anyway, they'll be too tired to run at the crackle of a slicker."

The fire died to a bed of coals, and a soft breeze moved over the land, and more stars showed now. Off in the night, the picketed horses were vague. The men began yawning. Loudon said, "Better hit the soogans, boys. Morning comes early."

One by one they obediently rolled into their blankets, all but Clem Latcher, who stoked up his pipe and took a walk off into the darkness. Loudon watched the fire wink out; then, on impulse, he rose and walked beyond where the men bedded and the horses stood picketed and found Clem, who stared into the northwest, over the miles they had come, standing with arms folded and pipe gone dead.

"A nice night, Clem," Loudon said.

Latcher nodded with no real interest.

Loudon asked abruptly, "What kind of man is Frome, Clem?" and asking, realized that this was what he had come out here to do.

Latcher seemed not to hear him at first, and then Loudon saw that he was pondering. At last Latcher said, "I'm not sure, Jess. A big man, yes, but a question bothers me: is he also a good man? He's built a big house. Because he needs one? Or because he wishes to impress his neighbors? He has many books. Does he read them, or does he just want to look scholarly? You see, these things can have two interpretations. And now he's got to stamp out the badlanders. What will it do to *him* to take the law into his own hands? You'll mind that I raised that point once before, at the steamboat landing."

"Yes," Loudon said. "I remember. What is it you're afraid of, Clem?"

"On a frontier, the good men make their own laws because there is no choice. It was so in the California diggings after the '49 rush. It was so in Bannack and Virginia City over twenty years ago, and in the Judith country just last year. After a while regular law replaces vigilante law. But in the meantime if a man hangs another for the good of everyone, what's to keep that man from hanging still another merely because the second man opposes him personally? You see, the self-appointed vigilante could learn how simple it is to eliminate opposition."

Loudon nodded. "Then Frome could take one trail or another . . ."

"This is a big country, Jess, and it's kind and savage at the same time. Kind because it holds promise and opportunity for the man who is big enough to meet the test. Savage because there is no law here but what we make, and the savagery in the land calls to the savagery in man. Who can say whether such a country will make or break any man?"

"I wonder if it will make *me,* Clem. Or break me."

Again Latcher was thoughtful. "I'm not sure I can answer that, either, Jess. I liked seeing you feed those hungry Indians this morning in spite of Corbin's reminding you that your action wouldn't please Frome. When you're your own man, you're a good man."

Loudon asked, "Do you think his giving me the foremanship was a bribe?"

Latcher shrugged. "Who knows? Maybe the house is big because he plans on having a family someday. Maybe the books are there because he loves them.

Maybe when the last badlander is hanged, he'll cut down the gallows tree."

They were both silent then, and because there was nothing more to be said, Loudon turned away. "We'd best get to our blankets, Clem."

"Yes," Latcher said, but still he stood. He became aware that his pipe had gone out, and he lighted it and pulled hard on it. In that instant his face was clearly revealed, gaunt and lonely and brooding. He folded his arms again and stood looking to the northwest, looking across the distance, and now Loudon knew that he looked to where a house stood at the bend of a river and a woman waited for him in her own fashion. He knew then what had brought Latcher out into the night alone and what doubts tortured Latcher; and he wondered how Jack Ives put in his time this evening.

He almost said, "I'm sorry, Clem," but he remembered his campfire thought that no friendship could be based on pity. So he only said, "Good night," and turned back to where his men bedded.

Hot, Frome thought. Mighty hot, considering that the night before, it had rained hard; but now the air was breathless, and the blankets lay heavy on him. No stir of breeze at the open window of his bedroom; the curtains hung motionless. He wasn't drowsy, though he'd been up early enough because he'd had to see Loudon and his men off on the trail to Miles City. Couldn't be quite ten yet, but it seemed that he'd lain tossing for a dozen hours.

He thrust the covers aside and swung his legs to the floor and stood up. His long nightgown gave him the itch, so he shucked out of it. He stood naked in his bedroom and alone in his house. He wondered if he should go to the parlor and get a lamp lighted and try reading, but he was in no mood for that. He began dressing. A breath of open air was what he needed, he told himself. He went outside. No moon tonight, and only a handful of stars. One of the dogs came padding up to him and thrust its nose against his hand, but he shoved the animal aside. "Go lie down," he said sharply. He was surprised at his own irritability.

He walked toward the corrals. He looked into the far darkness and wondered where Loudon and the others slept tonight. Loudon was shaping up well as a foreman, he reflected; but standing here by the corral gate, he had a clear picture of Loudon chousing Joe McSween's horse away, and his irritability grew. Damn it, he should have stood up to Loudon that day in stronger fashion. But it was a finished matter now, no hard feelings lingering. Loudon was pleased with the foremanship, though he hadn't looked it this morning, just taking his orders and nodding and looking rather glum. Not as glum as Clem Latcher, though.

Latcher, who'd left a wife behind at the little hay-ranch up north.

Frome went into the corral and lifted a rope from one of the posts and got the rope onto his own saddle horse. Soon he had the gear fumbled into place. He'd led the horse out of the corral and closed the gate when someone shaped up out of the darkness and Grady Jones' voice reached him.

"That you, Mr. Frome?"

"Can't you sleep either?" Frome asked.

"Thought I heard a fuss out here." Jones was near enough now that Frome could see that the man had pulled a pair of pants over his underwear. "Taking yourself a ride, eh."

"It's better than tossing in bed."

"Want to go alone?"

Frome nodded. "Thought I might take a turn up

around the schoolhouse and see if my niece is showing a light." He wished he could see Jones' face more clearly. High cheek bones, and skin swarthy enough to hint of Indian blood. A man who talked little, but Frome remembered rumors about him, the hint that he'd heard the owl hoot. One thing, it took guts to be an outlaw. Maybe he should have made Jones foreman after all.

"Go back to bed, Grady," he said. "I'll be all right."

But when he'd ridden far enough north to be abreast of the schoolhouse, Frome kept walking his horse along, taking only a sidelong glance to be sure the building was dark. Beyond the school, he lifted his mount to a gallop. He had known at the corral where he was going; he had the woman on his mind again. He'd told himself once that he would walk wide of her, but he'd had nights of wild imaginings since and thrust them out of his mind only to have the fire still burn, as it had done tonight, like something moving underground. And so he had made up his mind.

Admitting this, he also admitted to himself that he'd been thinking of the woman when he'd suggested to Loudon night before last that Latcher could make a hand on the Miles City trip. And why not? After all, Latcher didn't count one way or another. If Clem Latcher were really worthy of his wife, there would be a door closed and barred against Frome at the end of tonight's riding.

That door was indeed closed when he reached the dark house at the bottom of the slant, and a dog raised a fury in the yard. Frome swung down from his saddle and took a minute to placate the dog. Then he tied his horse to the corral gate. He could smell the river; a breeze moved across its face and streamed through Latcher's yard and touched him, and he realized he was in a sweat. That damn' dog!

He walked to the door and knocked. He heard her call, "Come in."

He opened the door and stepped into the darkness of the single room. He knew from memory where each piece of furniture stood, and he made her out dimly, sitting bolt upright in the bed. Starlight came through a small window. He moved across the room and stood by the bed; she looked up at him, faintly smiling, and reached her arms up to him.

She said with a sigh, "I waited till eleven and then put out the light and went to bed."

She had known, then, that he would come? With that thought, some last sentinel in his mind whispered that once he'd wondered what her price would be. Never mind; he was a smart enough man to make the best of any bargaining, whenever it came. Not now, though; not now. He seated himself by her and put his arms around her and was done then with thinking.

12

Cowtown

LOUDON HAD PUT ANOTHER FULL DAY BEHIND HIM. He stood in the dusk before the door of a livery barn, while about him the pulse of Miles City throbbed, the streets aglow with bright lights, the jingle of spurs a steady music as men tramped to and fro. A lot of trail drivers in town these days. Men on the main street and men on the side streets. The storeroom of every livery barn was piled high with cowboys' bedrolls and chaps, while the men, long on the trail, cut the dust from their throats or bucked the tiger in the gaming halls before heading out. Some would go overland to Texas by horseback; some would head for Chicago with a shipment of beef cattle. Meanwhile, though, they'd make up for the dusty days. Loudon had turned his own crew loose to have their fling.

"Just remember that we start shoving cattle toward Long Nine at the crack of dawn tomorrow," he'd told them.

Man, but there'd been a slew of cattle on the bedding grounds along the Yellowstone today! Twelve thousand, Loudon had been told, most of them from the South—Texas and Old Mexico—though there were Westerns, too, cattle driven in from Washington and Oregon and Idaho.

Loudon had found the trail boss with the Long Nine herd and had a palaver with him. A lean man, that drover, bearded and smelling of the dust and sweat from many miles. Feeling akin to him, Loudon had thought of the Texas Trail. Westward the empire builders moved, some historians argued. But they were wrong, as Clem Latcher had pointed out in campfire talk just the night before. It was northward that destiny was moving, northward from Texas' depleted graze, northward from the ravages of a war now twenty years over but still unfinished in the hearts of some like Singleton. Gazing across that sea of weary cattle along the Yellowstone, Loudon had known what Clem Latcher meant.

Making the necessary arrangements with the drover, Loudon had felt a tug of pride because he spoke for Long Nine. The drover had promised him that five of the trail crew would stay on till the Missouri. The stock inspectors had ridden out and had a look around, making sure no strays had drifted into the herd, and thus the critters would be ready for the crossing come another morning.

The arrangements completed, Loudon had led his men back to town, loping past Fort Keogh where uniformed soldiers passed back and forth.

Loudon's bunch had wanted to tie onto a meal where a man had his feet under a table. Parting company from the crew at the livery stable afterwards, Loudon stood wondering if Miles City ever slept. Seemed a long time back to this morning, when they'd broken camp on Sunday Creek. Damned if they hadn't sighted buffalo in the dawn, about twenty of them, some last remnant of the northern herd. Made Loudon think of Ike Nicobar, who worried over what had become of the buffalo. Would seeing those few have pleased Ike or made him all the sadder, remembering how once the land had been black with herds?

Well, there was no use standing here mooning about Ike and the buffalo. He walked to Orschel's clothing store, where he got himself fitted with a good pair of California pants. Loudon had the pants wrapped, not meaning to give them wear and tear on the trail home. He'd wear them on some special occasion, and he thought of Elizabeth. He'd thought of her often since leaving Long Nine. It struck him now that he was eager to be back and seeing her again.

No closed doors in Miles City. A rich harvest time for the saloon men and the gamblers, and they were working day and night. Through doorways, Loudon glimpsed men four deep around tables where the barbered housemen presided. Coming abreast of still another saloon, Loudon turned in. Under a blue-gray curtain of tobacco smoke, men milled restlessly, their voices a steady hum above the click of poker chips. Loudon elbowed his way to the bar and waited to be served. The bartender had a rind of sweat on his forehead that glistened in the light.

Loudon asked, "Are they working you too hard, friend?"

"Cowboy," the bartender said, "for a week now I've had my supper sent in to me. In another week I expect to find a chance to eat the grub that's piled up. What are you drinking?"

Loudon took whiskey but was in no hurry about downing the stuff. It wasn't the liquor he'd wanted but a taste of the excitement of this place, this town, this cowboy capital of the north. He watched the bartender for a while and wondered what it was like to be a bartender. Same work each day, but new faces to make one day different from another.

Aimless thinking, this. Loudon guessed he was getting tired and should go back to the livery and flatten himself out in the hay. Every hotel room in town had been filled by the time they'd got here in late afternoon. He looked about, hoping for a glimpse of some of his own men. He had long walked alone; but there was in him at times like these a need for others, for friendship, for glass touched to glass. He remembered frolicking in Miles with Joe McSween. He saw Clem Latcher in a far corner watching a poker game with no great interest. Light touched the gauntness of Latcher's face and made it a skull-mask with shadowed eyes.

A cowboy came crowding up to the bar and elbowed in beside Loudon. He was Chip McVey, one of Singleton's riders.

"You're a long way from home, Chip," Loudon said.

"I'm reppin' for the boss," McVey said. "Hell, he's got cattle coming in, too, Jess." He was a youngster, McVey, with a shock of corn-colored hair that always showed beneath the sweatband of his hat. His face was taut tonight; he was a boy made important by a piece of news bursting within him. "Heard you were here. Been looking all over for you. Jack Ives is in Miles, Jess."

Oddly, the first thought Loudon had was that Clem Latcher had worried needlessly about how Addie might be faring when Clem had stood in the darkness beyond the first night's campfire and looked to the northwest. Then Loudon felt the tug of an old anger, but it didn't seem to move him much. Tired, he guessed. Too tired for trouble.

He tried sorting out his feelings toward Jack Ives

and found them made of two parts. One was his personal anger, born that day Elizabeth had been wounded and he'd stood off Ives from behind a pile of rocks; the other animosity came from Ives' being a badlander while he, Jess Loudon, was foreman of Long Nine.

"The hell with Ives," he said. He was mildly curious as to why Ives was here, but it didn't really matter. A bigger town than Craggy Point for a bigger spree? A change of women for a change of luck? Loudon thought of Ollie Scoggins dead, and his voice turned sharper. "The hell with Ives," he said again.

McVey said fiercely, "Just the same, I'm sticking close to you tonight."

Loudon wanted to laugh. Singleton breathed fire and so scorched the souls of those who rode for him. Or was it that youngsters like McVey dreamed up trouble whether its shadow lay dark or not? When you were young, you were someone walking out of the pages of Ned Buntline's paperbacked thrillers.

Loudon lifted his whiskey and downed it. "I'm of a mind to pile into the hay. Maybe I'll see you on the trail, Chip."

"I'm sticking with you," McVey insisted.

"Come along then," Loudon said.

Clem Latcher had moved away from the poker table and was nowhere to be seen. Loudon looked for him as he elbowed toward the door. He came out into the night, but still he had to fight his way among men, for the walk was jammed. He worked toward the livery barn; and once he'd turned a corner, the crowd thinned out. He found Chip McVey at his elbow, breathing hard. He'd already forgotten McVey until the youngster made his presence so plainly felt. Loudon strode on.

Suddenly the steady beat of Miles City rasped

against his nerves, and he was sick of the place. Glitter here, yes, but it was the same glitter one found in the fooforaw dresses of the painted women who called from dark doorways. Excitement here, too, but not the excitement of a dawn along Sunday Creek and the last buffalo lifting their shaggy heads to smell their doom. He wanted to be gone from here. He wanted to ride a big range beneath a big sky. He wanted to skin into those new California pants and go calling at the schoolhouse and sit silent with Elizabeth and try to reach out to her through silence. His stride quickened, and he turned another corner and saw before him a newly laid out park near Tongue River. Now he could see lifting cottonwoods and smell sage, and the night became clean and big.

He turned to McVey and said, "For Pete's sake, Chip, go on back and get on with your drinking."

And then the shot came.

It flared over there in the park, and instinct made Loudon swerve aside. He went down upon one knee, letting his bundle drop as he fumbled for his gun. He heard Chip McVey swear lustily, and McVey's gun blasted so close to Loudon's ear that he was deafened. Ned Buntline's boy, all right. Again a gun flamed in the park; anger rose in Loudon. Damned if he liked being a sitting duck! He got to his feet and started headlong toward the park, running in a zigzag fashion and calling himself a fool for his boldness. Who was playing Ned Buntline's dime thriller now?

One man over yonder? Or two? A shadowy figure moved across his range of vision. He tilted his gun toward that figure, but the man shouted, "Long Nine!" and he was astonished to recognize Clem Latcher's voice.

Loudon cried, "Clem, you damn' fool! Watch out!"

But Latcher was almost to the place where the shots

had been fired. Loudon made out a second shadowy figure. That would be Ives, standing with feet spread apart and his gun held ready. Ives' gun spoke again, and far behind Loudon, Chip McVey's voice rose in a shriek. But Latcher was diving at the knees of Jack Ives, and the two of them went down and were a tangle upon the ground. Then one broke free and went off at a staggering run toward Tongue River. Loudon didn't dare risk firing. He came panting to where the other man sprawled and cried, "Clem? You hurt?"

"No. Just shaken up."

Loudon darted past him. He peered ahead as he ran, but he could no longer see Ives. He paused and listened, trying to pick up the beat of boots. The sound came to him, too faint with distance to point any direction. Once again Ives had fought and run away.

Loudon turned back to where he'd left Clem. The man had pulled himself to a sitting position and was getting his breath back. "You sure you're not hurt?" Loudon asked.

Starlight gave him a look at Latcher's face and so gave him the answer. No hurt there, but only a terrible calmness, and Latcher said in a calm voice, "I was nearly ready for him. It was Ives. He stepped into the saloon when you were at the bar with McVey. He saw you and backed out fast. I knew what was up from what his face showed. I've been following him ever since, and I saw him cut ahead of you." He pulled himself to his feet. "You think his bunch plans on hitting at the herd on the trail home?"

Loudon shook his head. "He's here alone. I'm sure of that. His feud's personal against me; but if he'd had men with him, he'd have lined them up to help. That's the way he works. I learned that in Craggy Point weeks ago."

Latcher brushed himself off. It was Loudon's thought that he'd underestimated this man only the night before last, thinking Latcher to be less than solid oak. Latcher's wild charge against Ives had been as brave a thing as Loudon had ever seen. Then he had another look at Latcher's face and understood. The man was dead and had been dead for a long time—not burying dead, but dead in spirit. You couldn't tally a man for courage when that man didn't give a hoot whether he lived or not. Just the same, he owed a debt now, and he acknowledged it in his mind.

"That was McVey with you?" Latcher asked.

"God, yes! McVey!" Loudon had again forgotten the boy. He turned and started back to where McVey had been, and Latcher came along. They found McVey down on the ground, moaning softly and biting at his underlip. He had not called for help; that, too, was part of the damn' foolishness of youth, being nervy when it made no sense, suffering the way the book decreed.

"Where?" Loudon asked.

"In the leg," McVey said between gritted teeth. "His second shot or maybe his third. It was Ives, wasn't it?"

"It was Ives," Loudon said. "Clem, give me a hand with him."

And Loudon was thinking what this story would mean to Singleton. He could hark up a clear picture of Singleton before Long Nine's gallery, sitting his saddle and making his say about what would happen when a Rafter S man got winged. Loudon shook his head. Crazy, that a damn' fool thing like McVey's messing into a business not his own might set off a clean-up. And he knew now that he'd been hoping there'd be no big clean-up. He remembered his fear on the way to Castle Bend—the fear of what a man did to himself when he took up his gun against others. That fear had been sharpened by what Latcher had said just the other night about Frome and what could come of Frome's taking the law into his own hands. That held true for every man. Damned if it didn't.

Before he reached for McVey, he walked over and picked up the bundle from Orschel's and tucked it under his left arm. Pants for pleasure, or pants for war? From now on, they'd be cut from the same cloth.

13

Home Range

PETER FROME SHOVED BACK THE LEDGER ON HIS LITTERED desk and stared at the long columns blankly. Bookkeeping, he realized, was the one type of confining work that he usually loved. Nothing dull about the big, buckram-bound ledgers when they brought a host of memories. Here was an entry for a herd of cattle purchased; behind it lay the sense of triumph from a good deal put over. Here was a figure representing last fall's cattle shipment, no lifeless hen-scratching when he remembered the cheap hotels along Chicago's South Halstead Street and the stench of the stockyards nearby. Figures covering the growing payroll. A total representing his overall worth. Nice to watch that total become larger. It made a kind of monument. Why was it that he had no taste for the book work today?

Better keep his mind on business. He leaned back in his chair in this little room that was his office and made a tally on his fingers. Nearly two weeks . . . Time that new herd was eating Long Nine grass. Let's see, Loudon would have got to Miles City two or three mornings after leaving here. Likely he'd have taken delivery on the herd the day after and started the cattle across the Yellowstone. Dangerous, that crossing, but Loudon knew his business. Allow a day or two one way or another for good luck or bad, and Loudon should be spilling cattle on Frome acreage any time now and riding in to make his report. Loudon and his men—and Clem Latcher.

Frome drew the ledger toward him again and dipped pen in inkwell. He knew now what stood between him and concentration. He couldn't risk going to Latcher's again tonight. Too dangerous, with Clem likely to be swinging down from his saddle before the door. Besides, hadn't he told himself that he'd take a good long time about going back? He'd made that pledge after another secret visit, just night before last. There was Latcher himself to think about, but it was the woman who was really dangerous. She would have her price, and someday the bill would be presented. Marriage, after a divorce from Clem? Such scandal might well ruin his political chances in the Territory. Besides, he had no wish to marry her.

But, God, he was alive with the memory of her! And when he thought of Latcher's return and the door that would be closed to him, he began to feel frantic. What claim had a man like Latcher on such a woman? At times he'd pitied Latcher, but now his feeling was something else, not quite hatred but bordering on it. And knowing this, he knew how completely he'd lost the fight with himself.

Work! He would bury himself in work. If he must think of the woman, he must remember the price tag, too. Forget the stolen nights, and picture her at the head of Long Nine's table, where the Territory's great men should be gathered to dine. Say to himself,

"Senator, I'd like to present Mrs. Frome," and conjure how that would be.

Maybe a wall of time and distance would help shut out the constant thought of her. For a long while he'd planned a St. Louis trip—he wanted to talk to the bankers there about more capital—but if he were going to make the trip this season, he'd have to get started before ice closed the Missouri. The prospect of steamboat travel always pleased him more than the thought of catching the cars at Miles City. But, damn it, how could he leave Long Nine with this badlander trouble that might explode any minute? No fall roundup yet, or plans for one, because the ranchers couldn't even talk everyday business. No cattle shipment figure to jot in the ledger; no profit to estimate.

He flung down the pen. From the window he could see part of the ranch yard. Indian summer haze lay upon it. Grady Jones crossed his range of vision, tall and dark faced, walking with an easy, gliding movement, his toes turned in like an Indian's. Somehow the sight of the man irked Frome. These simple souls like Jones had no real problems—a full belly and a straw-filled tick to sleep on was all they asked of life. A snort of cheap booze and a couple of silver dollars to slip into the shoe of some painted hussy. He watched Jones till the man disappeared.

He wished he hadn't turned his mind to the badlanders. He intended to hit them and hit them hard, but he had the lesson of Castle Bend to remember. He'd do things right when the real clean-up came. And he had Elizabeth to remember, too, standing in the yard and accusing him before all his men of wanting to spill blood. Damned if that hadn't been a day of too many defiances—first Loudon and that matter of Joe McSween's horse, and then Elizabeth. He'd said nothing to her since about it; but whenever he thought of the coming clean-up, he thought of Elizabeth. Well, he'd see to it that the clean-up was rigged so that he was a man without a choice—so far as she knew. He was smart enough for that . . .

The sound of boots on the porch wrenched him from his thinking, and he heard a loud knock. Jones had been heading toward the front of the house, and Frome called out, "Come in. Here."

Jones came straight to the office. He paused in the doorway, putting one shoulder indolently against the frame. He smelled of sweat and horses.

Frome asked, "Well, what is it?"

"Singleton's riding this way," Jones said. "I picked him up with glasses. Thought you'd like to know."

"Thanks," Frome said. He closed the ledger. Now why the devil was Shad Singleton paying a call? To talk for trouble again?

Jones still leaned in the doorway. It struck Frome forcibly that more than the mere delivery of a message had brought Jones into the house. He asked impatiently, "Anything else, Grady?"

"Reckon Loudon will be back soon," Jones said. "And Latcher."

"Should that make a difference?" Frome demanded.

"Yes," Jones said. "To you. Latcher, I mean."

He was smiling. He had skinned back his lips from his teeth, and he looked for all the world like a coyote. Something cold touched Frome. He put both hands on the desk, palms down, and asked in a steady voice, "Just what are you driving at, Grady?"

Jones shrugged. "Hell, I'd make as good a foreman as Loudon."

"Perhaps you would."

Jones' smile grew. "I'm the kind who'd always be sure no harm came to you. I believe in watching out for the boss. That's why I didn't cotton to your riding off alone that night a while back when I found you at the corral. Too many badlanders around. So I followed you."

Frome felt his face turn stiff. He didn't trust his voice and let a good thirty seconds pass before he spoke. "And what about it, Grady?"

"Like I said, I'd make as good a foreman as Loudon."

Keep a cool head, Frome told himself firmly. He had here a man nowhere nearly so simple as he'd supposed; he was at the mercy of this man. He wet his lips with his tongue. "Takes a badlander to catch a badlander," he said and recognized the echo in his words. Loudon had said something like that the night they'd talked here in this house about the foremanship.

"True," Jones said. "But that shouldn't take forever."

"No, it shouldn't," Frome agreed. "Can you learn how to wait, Grady?"

Jones gave his free shoulder a twist. "All my life I've been waiting for one thing or another."

Frome stood up. He stepped toward Jones and put his hand on his shoulder and matched the man's smile, yet in this very instant he knew that he hated Jones. Frome said, "Just wait a little longer, Grady."

Jones canted his head. "Sounds like Singleton got here. Somebody's sure kicking up gravel out front."

"Yes," Frome said. "I'll have to go see him."

He stepped past Jones and worked his way through the house. Half his mind was still on Jones, the other half on Singleton. What had brought Singleton so hell-for-leather? Rafter S, he remembered, had also been taking delivery on a herd at Miles. Had something happened there, some incident that had reached Singleton's ear by sagebrush telegraph while Loudon fetched the same news a slower way? An attack on the trail, perhaps, with men wounded or dead? He thought of Clem Latcher stiff across a saddle, his body tarpaulin wrapped, and in spite of himself his pulse leaped. He flung open the door and stepped out upon the porch; Singleton was hauling on his reins. One look at the old Texan's face told Frome that trouble had fetched Singleton—bad trouble.

He'd had, Frome thought, enough of trouble for one day. Latcher's coming home . . . Jones' damn' blackmail . . . and now Singleton, the breather of fire. But the smart man would turn trouble to his own use, making it a tool to the hand . . .

The new herd made a nice picture against Long Nine graze, Loudon decided. From where he sat his saddle on a hilltop, one leg crooked around the horn while his fingers shaped a cigarette, he could look down upon the cattle they'd trailed from Miles. Texas longhorns, some of them; and there were Durhams, red, roan, and white, cow-generations removed from old England. Others, too, that were without name or strain, both having been lost by haphazard range breeding which meant they were crossbred, or worse, inbred. Nothing fancy in color or kind in this herd, but a year from now they would have gained tallow, and Frome could write another profit in his ledger.

Well, Frome could find no fault with the condition of the herd. The drive up from Miles City had been slow. One day the herd had made only nine miles, though on another Loudon had taken up the slack by pushing them a full twenty. No trouble finding water, with so many streams feeding the Musselshell. At the last, the regular Long Nine hands and the boys who'd signed on at Miles had all been eager to get on to the ranch and rest their saddles.

He could see those riders yonder. They had put the herd where he'd told them to, and now they were bunched up and heading toward the ranch buildings a couple of miles to the north. All but Clem Latcher. Clem also sat a saddle here on the hilltop, about fifty yards from Loudon. His shoulders were slumped; he sat staring at the cattle below and staring even farther north, perhaps, past Long Nine's buildings. Not with any sharp interest, though. Not with eyes that really saw. Loudon remembered how he'd seen Clem in Miles City as a dead man.

Loudon reined his horse over toward Latcher. "Coming, Clem?"

Latcher looked at him blankly.

"You'll be wanting to get on home," Loudon said, "but you better stop first at Long Nine and have a bite of supper."

Latcher shrugged. "I guess so."

Loudon sighed. He supposed he himself should be glad the journey was done and that in a few minutes he'd be loping toward the ranch to climb the porch and make his report to Frome. No trouble, he'd say. No trouble? Then why wasn't he in a mood to get on to the last step of his task? He'd already made up his mind to say little about that brush with Jack Ives. Jess Loudon had been the one Ives was gunning for, and Chip McVey had been only the innocent bystander that happened to stop a slug. Why the hell should a whole range go to war over that?

Just the same, he'd ridden all the way from Miles with a strange reluctance. Like a man riding toward something he didn't want to come to.

The last he'd seen of Chip McVey, the boy had been bedded down in a Miles City hotel with a strong smell of medicine to him and a doctor telling him to lie low for a while. Ives' bullet hadn't much more than busted skin, but the kid had lost blood. Chip had been wondering noisily when the hell Rafter S would be getting a wagon for him so he could make the return trip.

Face it, Loudon had thought there in the hotel room, knowing damn' well that now the lid would blow off for sure.

Each day on the trail he'd seen the dust of Rafter S behind him as Singleton's men moved their herd homeward, too. At night he'd ridden back far enough to see their campfire. Quite a comfort having a neighbor so near; the badlanders would think twice about raiding one herd with another close by. But he'd had something else on his mind, as well. He'd wondered if one of the Rafter S hands had maybe ridden ahead, carrying the news to Singleton about Chip McVey.

Loudon glanced now at Latcher. "You made a good hand on the trail, Clem. I'll tell Frome so."

Latcher looked across space, not seeming to hear, his face sad. Loudon had told him about how Singleton had come to Long Nine and made war talk; perhaps Latcher was bothered, as he was, by the thought of what could come. But when Latcher spoke, he said, "I've been thinking about Frome."

"I mind the talk we had," Loudon said. "The first night out."

"I've been turning it over ever since, Jess. I think I know now what it was I wanted to say. You know the badlands. You can ride out of this grassy country into rock and desolation. The change comes so gradually that you're almost astonished when you find yourself in the rough country."

"I know."

"Could it be that deep in all of us lies a badlands, Jess, somewhere beyond sight? Call it the wild streak that sleeps in the best of men, and women, too. Don't we all ride into those badlands sometimes? Most of us come back, scared a little by where we've been and what it would be like to really let go and stay there. But couldn't any of us go so far we'd never find our way back?"

Loudon shook his head. "You mean that might happen to Frome?"

"It might happen to anybody, Jess. And for each, his badlands is a particular thing. You remember my telling you in Craggy Point that I intended killing a man? That was me, going into my badlands. You know how Joe McSween went into his, and what came of it. I don't need to tell you about Addie's badlands and how deep she's gone into them."

"And my badlands, Clem?"

"How far would you follow Frome, Jess, just to keep that foreman's job? At what point would you wake up to find that you'd quit being your own man? And would you wake up in time?"

Loudon shrugged. "And what is it you think is going to happen to Frome?"

"I don't know, Jess. But there's a risk he is running. He turns savage in order to fight savagery. He rides into his badlands once, and then he does it again, deeper. What then, Jess?"

"I don't know," Loudon said. "I just don't know."

He looked across the sweep of country in the direction of the badlands, and in spite of himself, he shuddered. Then he nudged his horse and went riding toward the ranch. From the corner of his eye, he saw Latcher coming down the slant beside him. He wanted to think about Latcher's notion, but the more he turned it over in his mind, the less comfort it brought. And the shadow that had lain upon him ever since Miles was the darker for his thinking.

14

Suspicion

SATURDAY MIGHT BE THE DAY MOST SCHOOL TEACHERS looked forward to, Elizabeth thought, but for her it held only emptiness. With another Saturday here, she went about making her breakfast; but even as she worked, she found herself looking from the school-house window for the first of the children. Then, remembering, she made a face. No swaybacked horses plodding in this direction today, two and three children perched on each bony back. She sat down to her food, and loneliness swept her.

She had awakened depressed, she recalled, more depressed even than on that first morning at Long Nine. But now that she thought back, she realized that her depression had been growing across the weeks. Whatever possessed her? Here was the fall, beautiful and golden; strong morning sunlight slanted through the window and touched the benches and her desk and glinted on the brass bell with which she summoned the children. Why now, in Indian summer, was she constantly thinking of the coming winter, hearing its prophecy in the wind that hunted around the schoolhouse nights?

She shook her head angrily. Over three weeks now since she'd been to the ranch. Perhaps she should run away from loneliness by saddling up and making the ride. But she kept remembering Charley Fuller's visit. Charley had brought supplies to her a few nights ago and lingered by the stove awhile, full of news. Loudon had got back with the herd; the steers had trailed well and were fat as could be expected. It had been good news to her that Loudon had returned. The mention of his name had conjured up a picture of him, his face quiet and his eyes thoughtful.

But Charley had gone on to say that Shad Singleton had paid a call at Long Nine and told of trouble in Miles City between one of his hands and Jack Ives, and Singleton was done with pussyfooting. Plumb done. It was bound to be war now, a complete wipeout. And Charley had stared at the stove and said no more, but his Adam's apple started bobbing and his eyes looked scared.

She guessed she didn't want to ride to Long Nine today. It might mean watching from a window as she'd once done while men packed up grub and looked to their guns and Frome strode about the yard giving orders. Ollie Scoggins had been up in a saddle, but now Ollie slept deep beneath a headboard. She remembered how she had faced up to Frome just before Long Nine had ridden from the yard. There had been at best an armed truce between them since.

That was what kept her from Long Nine today and had kept her away on other Saturdays. She didn't want to see Peter Frome. But was she being wilful without reason? Once, sometime during that awful first day at Long Nine, she'd told herself she mustn't judge him. Not right away. But since then she'd kept remembering the inheritance he'd not shared with her mother, and to this she'd added three more samples of what seemed to be his opportunism—his using her wound as an excuse to go after Jack Ives, his making Loudon foreman, and his failure to see that the horses taken at Castle Bend were restored to their rightful owners.

She stared at her coffee cup. Loudon had explained about the horses, defending Frome that rainy night nearly three weeks ago. Yet her feeling about Frome went deeper than any judgment made by placing one incident alongside another. She frowned. All she knew for sure was that she sensed something deep in Frome not to her liking.

Just last week she'd had an opportunity to meet him on friendly terms, but she'd chosen not to. She'd put in a restless evening, reading by the kerosene lamp; then she'd saddled up and gone riding. North. She'd got to thinking Clem Latcher was with the crew on the Miles City trail, and that meant Addie was alone, too. She decided to call on Addie; but when she got to the crest of the breaks, she reined up, seeing the lighted house below and knowing suddenly that she was in no mood for Addie's chatter. That was when she heard a horse coming and moved off the trail, remembering that badlanders might be abroad.

But it was Frome. She recognized his bulk and the clumsy way he rode. She watched him head down the slant to Latcher's, going on some ranch business, no doubt. She might have hailed him and ridden on with him and back south again, but she hadn't. And even now she couldn't have said exactly what reticence had kept her silent and hidden.

Sitting here this morning, turning all these things over in her mind, she found that her breakfast had grown cold. She got up and poured more coffee and sipped it slowly. She'd better find something to occupy her day besides aimless thinking that always brought her full circle back to no real conclusion at all. What of those new curtains she'd been intending to make? And she'd been thinking about a Hallowe'en party for the children. The holiday was only a couple of weeks away.

Feeling more spirited, she did up the breakfast dishes and made her bed; by mid-morning she found herself singing. Then she heard the scuff of a horse's hoofs on the hardpacked yard, and her singing stopped short.

She realized how tightly her nerves were drawn. Thinking of war had keyed her up. But certainly no badlander would be riding here in broad daylight! Not with the Long Nine buildings so near. Then she thought, *Jess!* She ran to the window and saw Frome dismounting heavily.

He had come here only once in more than a month. Thus had he respected her unspoken wish to be alone. He'd seen to her comfort by being sure that supplies were always on hand, and sometimes he'd sent her trivial messages by the riders who packed those supplies. But now he was here, and she opened the door for him.

"Good morning," he said and took off his hat and stepped inside.

She was surprised to see that he was thinner and looked weary. Shadows lay under his eyes, and his mustache drooped. The last few weeks had done something to him, and in spite of herself pity welled in her. She said, "Won't you sit down?"

He shook his head. Where was the old arrogance, she wondered, the Roman-senator look? He gazed about the schoolroom. "I see you've made yourself comfortable here," he said. "Is there anything you need?"

Yes! her heart cried. *I need to be more sure of you!* But she said, "Nothing, thank you. Charley Fuller was out just the other night."

"I suppose Charley told you what happened at Miles City. And how Singleton feels."

"He told me."

Frome shook his massive head. "Shad has been riding from ranch to ranch. He'll soon have an army raised."

"Then there's no stopping it?"

"Only a slim chance." He sighed. "I'm making the most of that chance."

"You needn't do what Rafter S does!"

His face stiffened. "Elizabeth, there are matters nothing in your experience or background has prepared you to understand. Out here, a man stands with his neighbors or he does not stand at all. Singleton's fight is my fight. Really, I have no choice. When the others ride, Long Nine rides, too."

"But you spoke of a chance—"

"I've sent a man into the badlands. He left this morning from Long Nine. He'll represent the ranch, but he's not exactly part of the ranch, so that makes him perfect for the job. He's riding under a flag of truce to hunt out Jack Ives and carry my word to the badlanders. And my word is this: If they'll clear out before another sunrise, I pledge that neither Long Nine nor any other ranch will chase them. But if they stay, we'll go in there and stomp them out. Unless Ives is a complete fool, he'll choose to run."

"And the man—?"

"Clem Latcher. He rode down last night to borrow some tools. I looked at him, and the idea hit me."

She was glad. Latcher was cool and had a command of words to make him persuasive. But her gladness went deeper. It sprang, too, from Frome's humanity in seeking this last chance of peace; and, equally important, it sprang from his having come here to tell her what he'd done. She said, almost humbly, "Thank you, Uncle Peter."

He took a step toward her. He was like an old bear burdened by too much of winter, a blind, groping bear. He said, "Elizabeth, you've been against me. Oh, I know why; hitting the badlanders has seemed to you one more selfish thing—a protection of my own interests, nothing else. I hope you'll think more kindly of me now."

She swept her hand toward the empty table. "Stay," she urged. "I'll make fresh coffee, and we'll ride back to the ranch afterwards."

"There are things I have to do," he said, and turned toward the door. "Another day, maybe. Why don't you come to the ranch for supper tonight?"

She watched from the window as he mounted his horse. He was smiling, and oddly it was the self-satisfied smile of one who'd accomplished a purpose. What had changed his attitude so suddenly from the humility he'd just been showing? She saw that he rode north instead of turning back toward the ranch-house. She watched until he was out of sight, and then she turned from the window, disturbed. She would sew until mid-afternoon, she decided; then she would ride to the ranch. She put her mind to her needlework and made her scissors fly. Better this than too much thinking.

After a while, she took the curtain she had been stitching and held it up to the north window to be sure her measurements were right. Doing this, she gazed out in the direction Frome had ridden. She could see nothing but a reach of prairie, dun with autumn's fading colors. And suddenly she knew where Frome had gone.

To Latcher's, of course. To tell Addie why Clem hadn't come home last night. Addie would be wondering and worrying, but for Frome's thoughtfulness. That was it. And then a suspicion struck her so hard that it almost brought her to her knees. A terrible suspicion that came full-blown.

Oh, no! she thought.

Taken apart, her suspicion was made from many small things which had suddenly shifted to form a pattern. There was the day she had ridden to Latcher's and overheard Clem accusing Addie and the woman crying. Snatches of Latcher's talk came back to her. ". . . I'm not blaming you. I'm blaming him for taking advantage of you . . . He was someone who was in Craggy Point yesterday . . . Jack Ives? . . . You've got to tell me his name, Addie." She remembered her not wanting to be found there. Then there was Frome's riding to Latcher's the other night and again today. Frome, who had asked Clem Latcher to go to Miles City. Frome, who had chosen Clem to ride today on an errand that would take him far from home into danger.

Oh, she hated this thinking! Frome hadn't been in Craggy Point the day Addie and Clem had quarreled about. Frome had been on his way home from Miles City where he'd talked with the Stockgrowers' about the rustling trouble. Or had he? There was only Frome's word for that.

She had let the curtain fall to the floor. She began changing clothes, putting on her wide skirt; and then, moved almost by a will beyond her own, she went to the shed where she kept her horse. She fumbled blanket and saddle onto the horse and fought the bit into his mouth. She rode out, heading toward the badlands. She had to find Clem Latcher. She had to!

Even if she was wrong about Peter Frome—and she intensely wanted to be wrong—there was still another man to think about, a nameless man who might well be Jack Ives. A man who saw Addie Latcher secretly but wouldn't have to be furtive with Clem Latcher dead.

No, she couldn't shut out that possibility, no matter which way she twisted and turned her thoughts. Why hadn't she remembered that quarrel between Clem and Addie earlier today? Then she could have told Frome about Ives' name being mentioned. She could have made Frome see the danger that might await Clem, flag of truce or no. But now, harking up a remembrance of Addie's sobbing voice, she was shaken by the most horrible thought of all. Suppose there were *two* men who visited Addie secretly! Suppose one had sent Clem into the badlands and the other awaited him there!

She shook her head. *Crazy! Crazy!*

She raised her horse to a gallop and held him to this until he began to flag. Then she let him walk. She felt feverish, sick deep inside. She looked back across the distance she'd ridden so blindly; the schoolhouse was lost to sight. Around her spread a vastness of country; ahead lay the badlands.

What a fool she was, hoping to find Latcher in that jumbled country! Frightened, she cried out in her mind to Jess; she wished she'd gone to the ranch to get him. But Charley Fuller had said something about the venting of old brands on the delivered herd; likely Jess was out on the range working on that job. She pushed on till the shadow of canyon wall and eroded rock lay heavy upon her.

She supposed that Latcher was heading for Castle Bend. She'd heard that the cabin at the old wood yard had not been burned the day of the raid. She had only a vague idea of Castle Bend's location; some of her pupils were breed children from the fringes of the badlands, and she'd talked with them a time or two. She could only ride along, her hope dying with the day and her desperation growing.

She shivered. Sometimes she paused and listened hard for the fall of shod hoofs on rock, and once she cupped her hands to her mouth and called Clem's name till the echoes caught up the sound and mocked her. How far ahead was Clem? Two hours? Three? Had he already finished his mission and turned homeward?

Twilight came on fast here in the canyon bottoms. Twilight reached out and enshrouded her, and she felt scared. She forced the horse to the top of a ridge and picked a way along it. She found that by climbing she'd gained a full hour of daylight. Besides, she could look out along the prairie. Sunset light swept over the land so that everywhere the grass lay golden, almost green, as if spring rose again in the old stalks. Then the light slowly died; the grass turned gray and sullen; and her spirits, briefly risen, sank again.

She followed one ridge until she found easy crossing to another, but now night was beginning to creep down on her. Then, searching below, she saw movement.

A wolf? The form was shadow within shadow; it seemed too small to be a horse and rider. But it was indeed man and mount; she grew sure of this as she peered. Again she cupped her hands to her mouth and called. Was this wise, she wondered too late. Suppose it were not Clem but some lone rider of these wastelands! Why hadn't she fetched the gun that Jess had insisted she keep at the schoolhouse? But she didn't imagine she could point a gun at a man, much less pull the trigger.

Then an answering call came to her, faint with distance until the echoes cried it up and down. Clem's voice! She called, "Wait! Wait, Clem!" and began moving faster.

15

Where Danger Dwelt

TODAY LOUDON HAD COME TO A DECISION. HE WOULD TALK to Frome. Not as he had talked to the man a few nights back, making his homecoming report, but as one man to another. He would tell Frome the whole of what had happened at Miles City, making it clear that the thing between Idaho Jack Ives and Jess Loudon was personal and no cause for a big clean-up.

He had been out on the range these several days with the crew that had been picked to change the brands on the new herd. That job had to be done before the herd got scattered. There would be work a-plenty without that, come roundup time. Frome had told him that first night after the trail to take a rest; Grady Jones could oversee the branding. But Loudon had shaken his head. Roundsiding in a bunkhouse wouldn't help the worry that plagued him. Better to work. That way he could lose track of the days and what each day was bringing nearer. Saturday now, wasn't it?

Another day of sweating over a branding fire, hearing bawling cattle, seeing cowhands spilling loops, their lips moving as they cursed because of wasted time. Team roping those cowhands were, head and heel, stretching their catch and waiting for a hand to tail it down and hold while the venting iron was run and the Long Nine burned on fresh and pretty. Loudon spelled men while they smoked or had coffee. Branding three thousand head of steers was a chore, even with twelve irons in the fire and plenty of horses, men, and hemp. But with all the noise and heat to distract him, Loudon still couldn't escape the shadow of worry.

Damn Jack Ives for his quick gun at Miles! Damn Chip McVey for getting in the way of a bullet not meant for him!

The whole business reminded Loudon of a snowstorm he'd once watched. That was down in the mountains of southern Montana where he'd ridden with Ike Nicobar and Joe McSween a couple of winters back. They'd sat on a hilltop and looked across an expanse in which hills lay fold upon fold to the clear blue of an uplifting range. While they watched, a snowstorm built about those peaks, that soon were as hidden as though a curtain had dropped over them. And it had—a gray curtain. Then the snow wall advanced, blotting out first foothills and then the far plain sloping from the foothills and then the nearer country. Ridge by ridge, foot by foot, he watched that storm come upon him. Suddenly he felt that he stood in the path of something relentless, unstoppable.

And now, here on Long Nine, he'd been watching another kind of storm advance. When had the far peaks first become veiled? On that day he'd driven to Craggy Point to fetch Elizabeth home? Or was it that same night, when he'd searched the hills for Joe McSween, carrying a shovel along? Damned if the storm hadn't been well upon him when he'd led Long Nine to the ruckus at Castle Bend that had cost Ollie Scoggins his life. But even so panic hadn't yet swept Loudon; he'd first sensed the full threat at Miles when he realized what Chip McVey's wound would mean to Shad Singleton. And since then he'd watched the storm creep onward, until today he'd known that he must go to Frome in the hope that its full fury might yet be kept from engulfing them.

Dusk was coming on, and he lifted his voice to his crew. "Enough for today," he shouted. After a while they were bunched up and riding to the ranch, all but those who would night herd the cattle till the branding was done.

Damned if he didn't miss Clem Latcher, Loudon thought as he rode along. For nearly two weeks he'd lived night and day with Clem, though come to think of it, sharing campfires to Miles and back shouldn't make him lonely for Clem. Living together all of last winter hadn't made them what you might call brotherly. But Clem, too, had watched the storm coming. That was it. Few enough words they'd swapped about it; but both of them had known, and knowing, drawn closer together. He remembered how quiet Clem had been after the trail, when Clem had stopped at Long Nine for supper and talk buzzed of how Singleton had called again with blood in his eye.

Sure, the others were scared, too, the lean riders of Long Nine; but it was different with them somehow, not going so deep as with him and Clem.

Frome wasn't at the ranch when the branding crew came in, so Loudon ate in the cook-shack with the men. Tonight a half dozen Looped L hands were here taking supper with them. They'd ridden in during the afternoon, Loudon gathered, and nobody was asking them their business on Long Nine. No need. This was the beginning of a massing of riders from all the ranches. The table talk, rattling on, was just words flung into the air to fill it up. Grady Jones seemed the only man who had a full appetite. Loudon studied him. Did Jones' kind hanker for violence?

After supper, Loudon asked Sam if Frome had yet showed back. The cook shook his head. "Where did he go?" Loudon asked.

"Rode north. This morning."

"Alone?"

"Yup."

Loudon said angrily, "He shouldn't be doing that."

He wondered if he should saddle up and go looking for Frome. Damn the man for his carelessness! Loudon went into the bunkhouse and watched a poker game get started. He went outside and paced the yard for awhile. Long after dark, Frome rode in and swung down from his saddle.

Loudon went to him. "Got a minute?" he asked.

Frome looked tired. Sour, too, as though it had been a bad day. "Something about the branding? You can tell me later."

Loudon said, "It's not that. It's about the trouble. Do we have to ride into the badlands again?"

Frome shook his head. "No telling. But we're down to our last chance."

"You mean there *is* a chance?"

"A slim one. I've sent Ives word that if his bunch clears out, we won't take their trail. Latcher went looking for him today under a flag of truce. Has Clem showed back yet?"

Loudon heard his own voice shouting. *"Clem?* You sent *Clem* to Ives?"

Frome took a backward step. "Man, what the hell's the matter?"

Loudon wanted to hit him. He doubled his fist and half raised it before sense swept through him like a clean wind. Frome hadn't known! Damn it, Frome hadn't known! Loudon shook his head. "It's my fault. I should have told you before. Ives has reason to want Clem dead."

"Latcher said nothing about that to me."

"He doesn't know."

Frome said, "I just don't see what this is all about, Jess."

"A personal thing. I aimed to tell you tonight so you'd savvy that Ives' tackling me in Miles was personal, too. It's Latcher's wife. She's been Ives' woman. Ives knows that I know it."

Frome said, "Eh? How's that?" His hands began shaking. "I didn't know," he said. "Believe me, Jess, I didn't know."

Of course you didn't, Loudon thought. Yet there was something in Frome besides regret. There was no name for it, but it was there, deep in his eyes.

Frome said suddenly, angrily, "Put yourself in my boots, Jess. I tried war, and it cost me Ollie. Then there was the shooting in Miles. Not that that really mattered; sooner or later some stray spark would have struck the powder. The ranchers are bunching their hands here, since we're closest to the badlands. We've no choice left. Unless Clem comes back with word that Ives is willing to run. Clem was the only hope I had."

Loudon said fiercely, "He'd better come back."

Frome took a stride toward the house. "If Grady's around, tell him I want to see him," he said.

Loudon nodded. He began walking toward the

corral, but halfway there he stopped. No sense in snaking out a horse and riding into the badlands. Not now. Too many hours had slipped away. Whatever had passed between Clem Latcher and Jack Ives was done with. Nothing left but to hold to a last, feeble hope that Clem would indeed ride back and bring with him the right word. Otherwise the storm would catch up and engulf them all.

Grady Jones—? Frome had wanted Jones sent to him. It seemed that Frome thought often of Jones these days. Loudon turned toward the bunkhouse to find the man.

Enough light still grayed the sky to show Elizabeth Clem Latcher's face when she'd picked her way to where he waited in a canyon bottom. A calm face. Elizabeth tried to match his calm, but not till now had she thought what she would say when they met. How could she tell him that she feared for him because she'd come to believe that another man, perhaps two, coveted his wife?

Latcher asked, "What are you doing out here, Miss Bower?"

"Just riding," she said. "And then I got lost." She let out her breath. "I was never so glad to see anyone in my life!"

"You must have very sharp eyes," he said. "You recognized me from the ridge. You called my name."

She flushed. He seemed to be studying her, quietly, reflectively, and she hadn't fooled him one little bit. Of course not. To cover her awkwardness, she said hurriedly, "Let me stay with you."

He shook his head. "I might be all night. I'm looking for a man. I wasted a lot of daylight by going to Craggy Point first, thinking he might be there. Sorry."

"I *must* stay with you!"

He pondered. Finally he said, "If you don't want to ride alone, I'd rather you'd wait here for me."

Perhaps there was a chance for him if she stayed by his side. Perhaps her presence could make the difference when he found his man. Then, too, there was the crowding night, and not far away, the lonely voice of the river. She shivered. Her mission was somehow submerged in her fright, and thus his need and her own were mixed and had become one.

"Please!" she begged. "Please take me with you!"

Again she felt that her mind lay open to him and that her fear for him was showing as plain as her fear for herself. She wished he wouldn't stare at her so steadily.

"Very well," he said at last. "On one condition. Any order I give you must be obeyed without argument. If I tell you to stop at a certain point and wait, you must do so. If I say to go, you're to turn and leave me. No matter what the circumstances. Do you understand?"

"I understand," she said.

He reined his horse about and started in the general direction of the river. She rode behind him, keeping her eyes on his back. When full darkness came, she was guided by his voice. "Turn right now. . . . Turn left."

Soon they reached the river. Across it high rocks loomed, ghostly in the first starlight; and close by, on this side of the river, other rocks rose, but here there was a shelf of land. They moved steadily downstream. That they were following the river was the only thing she knew for certain. There was no compass in this black world, no time, and no distance.

She found herself marveling at Latcher's unerring

instinct as he moved along. These badlands he had not learned from books. He must have ridden them often, and she wondered what strange pull they had for such a man. In her, too, grew admiration for his courage. He had been sent upon a mission that at best held danger, and he moved forward unflinchingly. She wished the riding done.

Finally his voice came back. "Easy, now," he called. "Stop where you are and wait." And hard after that another voice that was not Latcher's said harshly, "Hold up there!"

Silence.

Then she heard Latcher say, "I've got my hands up. Don't get jumpy, man. There's a girl with me. We come in truce."

The harsh voice said, "Don't so much as bat an eyelash."

Silence again. Silence and darkness till Elizabeth caught the scrape of boots on rock and glimpsed lantern light that vanished and reappeared as the lantern moved among great rocks. Shortly the lantern became a blinding brightness within a few feet of her. She saw the shape of the man who held it aloft and was certain that other men stood behind him. The lantern was being flashed in Latcher's face, and the man who held it shouted, "Come up here, girl."

She understood now that Latcher had waited just a minute too long. He'd known they were nearing the badlander hideout, and so he'd told her to wait, for he'd not intended to take her in with him. What he obviously hadn't expected was sentries. Now the lantern was flashed upon her, and one of the shapes behind the lantern found astonished voice. "By God, it's Frome's niece!"

Someone moved up to Latcher and placed hands upon him and said, "Hell, he's not carrying a gun."

Elizabeth said, "Neither am I," and no move was made to search her.

The man with the lantern said, "Come along, both of you," and began backing away. Elizabeth urged her horse up beside Latcher's. In the lantern light, his face looked rigid. Men closed in around them, and they moved up a slight slope, picking their way among the rocks. Ahead, she dimly made out a cabin and a stable and a corral. So this was Castle Bend! Just as the Long Nine riders had described it when she'd forced talk from them of that hideous evening they'd spent here. In these rocks, Ollie Scoggins had died. She shuddered.

The cabin door was flung open as they neared the building, and a man stood in the doorway, silhouetted by the lamplight behind him. She recognized that high, waspwaisted figure.

Ives, peering, asked, "Who have you got?"

"Clem Latcher. And Frome's niece. Come under a truce, they say."

Ives stiffened. He remained a blackness against the light until the man with the lantern got closer. Ives' face was handsome; also, it was blank. He'd been a gambler, she remembered. She looked about her in the lantern light and saw at least half a dozen men, and she sensed that there were more in the cabin and more in the outer darkness. She tried to recognize the rustler she'd once knocked from his horse. Ives was looking at her. He was a man appraising a woman; but more than that, he was one breed of person studying another, gauging her strengths and weaknesses. He smiled slightly. "A little different from our last meeting," he said.

"Yes," she said. "You had a gun in your hand that time."

"The shooting was only to scare you into stopping. We didn't mean for you to be hit. Shooting women isn't my style."

"You were trying hard enough after Jess Loudon showed up!"

Ives frowned. "That was another matter. The bullets were for Loudon then." He looked at Latcher, and his voice took on a sharper edge. "Well, Clem, what is it?"

"Frome sent me, Jack. His word is that if you and your bunch will clear out, he'll give you no chase. But if you stay, it's a clean-up."

Ives asked, "And he sent the girl along?"

"No," Latcher said. "She went riding and got lost. Her trail happened to cross mine. There was nothing to do but bring her along."

Ives said with hard conviction, "She didn't get lost. She trailed after you."

"We needn't be concerned with that, Jack. Frome will want an answer."

"Frome," Ives said, "can go straight to hell."

Latcher shook his head. "Jack, you'd better remember what happened to the rustlers in the Judith clean-up last year." His face saddened. "Man, I'm trying to do you a favor!"

Ives said, "You weren't always so damn' considerate, friend. What I'm remembering is the way you busted into my play at Miles City. I've been looking forward to the time I'd lay eyes on you again."

His talk of Miles had to do with what had happened there between him and Jess Loudon, she supposed—the shooting Charley Fuller had told her about. But it struck her that Ives was trying to make a case against Latcher beyond the simple facts, and by turning the talk to that, Ives had as good as torn up the invisible flag of truce. Ives' men knew it. Something ran through them that turned them still-faced. Someone's boot sole scraped against rock, and from the corral Elizabeth could hear the stomping of horses. She felt disembodied at this moment, yet intimately concerned, as though she stood on a yonder ridge watching herself in the midst of these men and yet at the same time was here, feeling their temper catch fire from Ives' and reach out to scorch her and Latcher.

Latcher shrugged. "I've got to carry your word back to Frome. Next time, we can take up whatever is personal between us."

Ives said, "The girl can carry back the word."

Elizabeth looked straight at him. "I came here with Mr. Latcher; I leave only with him. Have you forgotten the truce, Mr. Ives?"

Ives stood silent, and she could see that he made a fight with himself. And watching him, she became certain that it was his name Addie Latcher had withheld the day Clem questioned her. For Ives wanted Latcher dead, and that desire went deeper than what had happened in Miles City. But something else showed in his taut face—something that grew as he looked at her. Again he was one breed of person estimating another; and she knew him thoroughly then. He fancied himself a gentleman, and that pretense was dear to him, so dear that he did not want to be revealed to her as counterfeit. This was his vanity, and her appeal to honor had played upon it.

"Let them go," he said.

Latcher flicked the reins and moved his horse, and Elizabeth did likewise. Something like a collective sigh ran through Ives' men; and then the circle opened for the two as they picked their way toward the river bank. Almost at once they were swallowed by darkness, and in darkness they began moving upstream. Neither spoke. Latcher led the way, and after a while he turned south from the river and headed between canyon walls. Elizabeth found herself shaking. After a long while they came out upon prairie. A sliver of moon was rising to the east above the badlands.

Latcher reined up and listened intently. Elizabeth listened, too; she could hear no sound of pursuit. She wished Latcher would speak, say something—anything—but he didn't. They began riding again.

He brought her to the schoolhouse. Evidently he was intent on riding on to Long Nine's buildings, but at parting he drew rein. In the starlight his face was weary and sad. There was, she sensed, something he wanted to say, but it took him a long moment before he said it.

"Thank you, Miss Bower."

He knew. What she had known at Castle Bend he had realized, too, for Jack Ives' face had been as readable to him as to her. It was not for saving his life that he was thanking her, but for the keeping of the wordless secret that lay between them and had really been there since they'd met beneath the ridge and she'd given him a lie in answer to his question. Now pity rose in her, and she wanted to say something that would comfort him, but still there could be no words. There could never be words. The sore in him was not to be touched.

She tried to smile. "Good night, Clem."

She watched him ride away, and then she put her horse up and hurried into the schoolhouse and closed the door and put her back to it. She had the feeling that she was fleeing—fleeing from what she had seen in his eyes at the last. From that, and from something else awfully present but as yet not recognizable. She only knew that she felt terribly lonely and terribly afraid. Then she remembered the word that Latcher was carrying to Frome, the report of failure; and she knew then what the second terrible thing had been that had happened tonight. Not till now had she thought of the mission and its consequences.

16

Eve Of Disaster

IVES! IVES! IVES!

To Frome, seated in the ranch-house kitchen with his supper turned cold before him, the name kept beating in his mind, as it had ever since Loudon had spoken to him in the yard an hour before. Lord, but Loudon had as good as kicked the legs out from under him. "It's Latcher's wife," Loudon had said. "She's been Ives' woman." The news had taken Frome's appetite away.

Ives! That—that cheap tinhorn gambler! That sneaking dark-of-the-moon rustler! To think that she cared for a man of Ives' shoddy cut when her first choice could have been him, Peter Frome. What made the woman such a fool? He was disgusted with her; he never wanted to see her again. But even as he told himself this, he knew that he would go back to her. Damn it, he'd go back if for no other reason than to give Ives a run for his money.

Small wonder that Addie had been hesitant this afternoon. He remembered his impatient assurances to her that Clem was far away on Long Nine business and so beyond worrying about. Even so, she'd kept saying, "I'm afraid . . . I'm afraid . . ." Not because of Latcher only, he knew now. No, damn it! There was still another rider who might have come down the slant after seeing the corral empty where Latcher's horse usually lazed.

Ives!

The man had been gone to Miles City at the same time that Loudon's crew was there, Latcher with them. So that's why Addie Latcher's door had been open to Peter Frome! How it graveled him to realize that! But Ives had doubtless since returned to the Missouri. Addie had known he was back, you could be sure. That's why she'd been so different today.

Lord, but he'd looked forward to the visit! Half of his reason for sending Latcher into the badlands had been to provide such an opportunity. He'd been honest with himself about the whole thing, damn it, then and now. True, he'd considered that badlander temper might be such that Latcher would never ride back, flag of truce or no. But he'd impressed that danger on Latcher. "You realize the risk?" he'd kept asking Latcher.

He could clearly remember the wooden way Latcher had nodded his head. Well, if Latcher were dead now, no man could accuse Peter Frome of having forced him to his death. Latcher had been willing to ride. And one last attempt at peace had been necessary; thus Elizabeth wouldn't be standing in the yard with accusations when again Peter Frome led Long Nine's riders on a foray.

Elizabeth—? Where was she tonight? There'd been no light in the schoolhouse when he'd reached it, coming south from Latcher's; and he'd looked and seen that her horse was gone from the shed. He'd been sure then that she'd gone on to the ranch for supper, as he had proposed; but most obviously she wasn't here. What did that mean? Surely she had stood convinced of his good intentions at their parting. He'd kept his face well schooled. Could it be that he hadn't fooled her, after all? He shook his head, growing angrier.

Quite a lot of commotion out in the yard. Riders had come in while he was toying with his supper—Boxed C, Cottrell's outfit, Sam had said. Now a new batch clattered in from somewhere. Quite an army building up. Singleton would probably be striding into the house before midnight, wanting to make war plans. Well, he'd ride with Singleton. Whether Latcher brought the right word or the wrong one, there'd be a clean-up. He was suddenly eager to be at it.

Was this because of what he now knew about Ives? Hell, it didn't matter. If he hated Ives because the man stood between him and Addie Latcher, the fact still remained that Ives was first of all a rustler who had to be stamped out.

He thought about hate. A strong emotion, he decided, and therefore worthy of a strong man. In a way, he hated Clem Latcher, too, though perhaps what he felt for Latcher was made more of contempt. The difference in one hate and another was only a matter of degree, a thing tempered by various circumstances. Take Loudon. He'd hated the man that day Loudon had defied him over Joe McSween's horse, but Loudon had been too valuable to run off the ranch.

That was it. A wise man rode his hate instead of letting it ride him. That was why he had sometimes since forgotten his hate for Loudon, yet it had persisted. Certainly when Grady Jones had spoken some days ago about wanting the foremanship, he'd remembered how Loudon had defied him. He hadn't remembered right away, but he had remembered.

Grady Jones he despised. The man overestimated his power; and he'd been more than insolent since that set-to in the office. Right now, Jones was keeping him waiting, for it must be more than an hour since Loudon had been sent to find Jones. Stirred, Frome got up and opened the kitchen door and peered out into the yard. A little moonlight now. Black shapes moved about. A quiet bunch, considering how many men were crowded here tonight. Frome raised his voice to a yell. "One of you, tell Grady Jones I'm waiting for him."

The irony was that he didn't really want to see Jones. He'd made it a point to show Jones special little attentions lately; it was a way of keeping the wolf at bay. After a while, Jones came in. He left the kitchen door open behind him and grinned at Frome, and then poured coffee for himself from the stove. He brought the cup to the table and sat down.

Frome said coldly, "You were slow enough about coming."

"A poker game in the bunkhouse," Jones said. "Outside money, too. Those Looped L boys are packing summer pay."

Frome thought, *How badly do I need this lout?* and his anger rose so high that he was afraid it showed.

Jones asked, "Latcher not back yet?"

"Not yet."

Jones grinned. "How you bettin' that he won't come back?"

Something inside Frome exploded. The man didn't need to bring up Latcher's name every time they talked. "Damn it, Grady, I sent Latcher because he was our last chance. What other man could possibly get to Castle Bend?"

"Sure," Jones said. "Sure. Clem was the natural choice. No need to get hot about it." He yawned and stretched his legs out. "Plenty riders bedded in the barn. How long you going to be feeding that army?"

"Breakfast tomorrow," Frome said. "And then we ride."

Jones' eyes glinted. "Regardless?"

Frome hesitated. He felt pushed—pushed by Jones and by his own anger. "We'll see what Latcher has to say."

Jones said, "You put too much trust in him. I wouldn't trust any small rancher."

"Meaning—?"

"You ever know a small rancher who ate his own beef?"

"Latcher's honest," Frome said.

"Maybe," Jones said. "It's something to think about, though." He sipped at his coffee. Frome watched him. What was it, really, that Jones was driving at? Then Jones tilted his head toward the kitchen door, listening intently. "Somebody's rode in," he said. "I just heard a name shouted. More neighbors?"

Frome went to the door and peered out. Again he could see nothing but black shapes, but as he peered harder, it seemed to him that only one man was dismounting by the corral. A tall shape came toward the house. "It's Latcher," he said; and his feelings were mixed—curiosity and doubt—yes, and a sharp pang of disappointment, too.

"Ah," Grady Jones said. "Now we'll know."

Loudon, from the bench beside the bunkhouse, saw Latcher come riding in; and with the man stepping down from his saddle, he knew how hard he'd been watching for Clem. Earlier, Loudon thought he had shut his mind to Clem, not wanting to fret where fretting would do no good. Just the same he'd perked up his ears each time hoofs beat against the prairie and strained his eyes to scan each group of riders who'd come in.

Mostly he had just sat, saying a howdy to any of the neighbors who happened to come near him, watching the dark shiftings as men roamed the yard, seeing some of them go to the barn to bed down. Through the open door of the bunkhouse, he had heard the sounds of a big poker game going on and wondered when Grady Jones was going to throw in his hand and head for the house and Frome. Jones had been in no hurry, not leaving till a short while ago, after Frome had shouted from the kitchen.

No sign yet of Shad Singleton. Singleton would be the trigger to a loaded gun. But likely Singleton was still out recruiting, riding from one ranch to another and telling the boys to bust the breeze to Long Nine and be ready for the kill. A few Rafter S hands had ridden in not long ago, but their big boss hadn't been with them. One of those hands was Chip McVey.

That surprised Loudon some. He had watched how awkwardly Chip got down from his saddle and how stiffly Chip walked. That wounded leg was likely giving Chip considerable pain. He had come limping toward the bunkhouse, and Loudon said, "Evening, Chip. Sure didn't expect to find you putting your weight against a stirrup."

"Hell," McVey said, "I got a personal stake in this clean-up, you'll recollect."

Loudon had to smile. Ned Buntline's boy to the finish.

"Better take it easy, Chip. That leg of yours hasn't had time to heal."

"I don't shoot with my leg," Chip said, and touched the gun against his thigh. "Don't you go wastin' any worry on me, pard. I'll make a good enough hand when the time comes."

Loudon watched him limp on into the bunkhouse and then heard McVey's voice raised in there. A sure enough dyed-in-the-wool eighteen carat hero.

Later, a little later, Clem had come.

Heading for the house, Clem walked like a tired man, not even cutting a straight path from corral to building. He veered far enough to one side to walk through the splash of light that fell from the bunkhouse door, but he didn't see Loudon. Loudon looked at him and didn't speak. Latcher's very presence told him that Clem had come out of the badlands unharmed; Latcher's face told him the rest. Clem wasn't fetching good news.

Latcher gone on toward the house, Loudon stood up. He was done, suddenly, with this bench he'd warmed so long, this yard with its restless movement, this night with its voiceless threat. He was done with seeing men come in to fill bunkhouse and barn, taut, silent men not liking what lay ahead but no more able to change things than the hills had been able to stop that storm he'd seen from marching across them. Loudon went to the corral and snaked out his own horse and saddled up. He rode north out of Long Nine's yard.

He had no destination in mind. He only wanted to be out in the night and the feeble moonlight, and as soon as he'd wrapped full lonesomeness around him, he felt better. The stars had a cold look; a breeze ran close to the land; and somewhere, distantly, he heard a coyote lament. The thought struck him that he could just ride on. This was his own horse, bought from wages. Nothing tied him to Long Nine, really; nothing said he had to take part in what was coming. Yet he couldn't run from reality. He shook his head and rode on aimlessly.

After a while he saw the light of the schoolhouse across darkness, and he headed for the building. Had he been heading this way all along? He couldn't have said for sure; he only knew that he was glad Elizabeth was still up. He put his horse in the shed; and when he raised his hand to rap on the schoolhouse door, he remembered he'd meant to wear his new California pants when he came calling here.

She opened the door and stared at him like someone roused from sleep. Her hair was awry as though she'd been pushing her hands through it. She said, "Come in, Jess."

He stepped inside and at once felt thick-tongued, not sure what he was going to say now that he was here. He could bring her no news but bad news, and she didn't look ready for that. Or rather, she looked like she'd already had it.

"Evening, Elizabeth," he said.

"You've been a long time getting here, Jess."

"I wanted to come," he said, and realized now why he hadn't; there could be no easy talk between them, not with the way things were. "I've been meaning to come ever since I got back from Miles." And now he said all that was left to say. "It's here, Elizabeth. You might as well know. Frome sent Latcher to try to make a bargain with the badlanders. Clem failed."

"Yes," she said. "I was with him."

He supposed this should surprise him, but it didn't. He didn't even feel like asking her how she had happened to go into the badlands, too. The whys and the wherefores had quit mattering. It was only tomorrow that mattered.

She asked, "How is it at the ranch?"

"Riders from everywhere," he said. "They've been gathering all day." Or was it Frome she'd really asked about? "I guess your uncle's just been waiting till Clem got back."

"Oh!" she said and swayed slightly.

Then she was into his arms. He couldn't have told whether she had taken the full step between them or whether he'd gone to meet her. It didn't matter. He only knew that she was hard against him and his arms were around her. He held her tightly. He kissed her and began stroking her hair. He spoke to her, saying her name over and over.

"Jess," she said, her voice muffled, "will you ride away?"

"Will you go with me?"

"I can't," she said. "There's a thing I've got to find out for sure."

"Frome, Elizabeth?"

"Frome."

"I'm tied, too," he said.

He knew now what held him; it had been there since that day the steamboat had landed and he had gone aboard looking for her. Another day in Craggy Point, the day after Joe McSween had died, he had wondered about this girl and Frome and sensed that she was troubled. Ever since then, he had known that she might need the strength of his arm, and on a rainy night in this very building he had wanted to come closer to her. And now both of them were held fast. Odd how things got twisted around. That day on the boat he had asked her to turn back from what lay ahead; tonight she was asking him.

Now she was shuddering. She pressed harder against him and whispered, "Jess! Oh, Jess!"

The warmth of the room lay heavy upon him. There

was her soft breathing and the smell of her hair. There was the movement of wind against the wall, and the beating of his own heart. There was the oneness between them—this great goodness that had come out of a night that had held no goodness. He said, "I'll be here tomorrow, Elizabeth. There will never be any riding out unless you ride with me."

17

A Clump Of Cottonwoods

EARLY MORNING LIGHT SMARTED LOUDON'S EYES, AND THE clamor of the yard beat against his ears; but his mind seemed numb, as though he couldn't rightly get hold of these doings. Same old thing of men gathering up guns, with Frome everywhere, chaps on and a gun buckled at his side. A lot more men involved this time, though. Between forty and fifty, Loudon judged. Singleton's men and Lathrop's and Cottrell's, and a few other ranches', too. Enough generals to go around, with Singleton barking orders and Buck Lathrop and Ab Cottrell here. Sunlight flashed on the hides of skittish horses as men rose to saddle.

Frome would lead the whole army. That had been decided last night, Loudon guessed, after Singleton arrived. No water bags for this ride. No sacking carried along to wrap the horses' hoofs. The sun hadn't much more than cleared the horizon; the chill of fall was in the air.

Took this bunch an ungodly long time to get ready.

Some were still at breakfast in the cook-shack—they'd had to eat in relays. Others were fighting horse and gear. What talk there was came low voiced, save for Frome's shouted orders and the barking of Singleton. Nobody was any happier about this frolic than Long Nine had been about Castle Bend. Even Chip McVey looked now like he wished he was somewhere else.

Tex Corbin edged his horse up beside Loudon's and said, "What do you make of it, Jess?"

Loudon said, "We'd do better with half as many men moving twice as fast."

Grady Jones rode by them, his lips peeled back in a grin. "Good day for hunting," he said. Jones was the one man looking pleased by the prospect. What was it Clem Latcher had said about the wild streak that slept in men?

Charley Fuller sat a saddle, hunched and miserable. He looked toward Loudon and tried to grin.

Frome shouted, "Long Nine! Over here!" He circled with his arm.

Gradually the crews got bunched and ready, Long Nine and all the rest. Frome lifted his arm in a forward wave, and they rode out of the yard, a shapeless army. They headed almost due north. Loudon found himself hemmed in by others. He was not the man at the head this time; he was just one more rider carried along. He wondered now if something in him had willed his mind to numbness. He remembered Clem's asking, "How far would you follow Frome, Jess . . . ? At what point would you wake up to find that you'd quit being your own man?" Clem wasn't with them today, which meant that Clem had gone back to his river-bottom ranch after he'd made his report to Frome last night. No real call for Clem to ride. Thank heavens for that.

Nobody in the school yard when they rode past the place. Too early, Loudon supposed, and then a thought struck him. *My God, it's Sunday!* He wondered if Elizabeth was looking from the window. He didn't glance that way to make sure. They had found each other last night, and he didn't want the goodness of that changed by what her face might show now, watching this army ride past.

He stared fixedly at the back of the man just ahead. One of Looped L's riders. He looked out across openness, the great distance that spread emptily to the Missouri. He looked to the hills where once he'd searched for Joe McSween and was reminded that he'd meant to go back and mark Joe's grave. He didn't want to think about Joe. A lot of familiar things along this road, the bleached bones of buffalo, the occasional sky-lined antelope. How many times had he traveled this way? After a while he began to wonder when they would veer toward the badlands. He asked about this.

"Craggy Point," someone told him. "The bosses got word that the badlander bunch moved there last night and holed up."

Singleton, that wily Texan, would have had scouts out, of course. Well, Ives would have had his own scouts at work. Craggy Point? As good a place as most to fort up for a fight, but the badlands were better for hiding. Now why the hell had Ives moved his men to the settlement? Then he knew. Ives, too, was done with watching the storm creep closer. Every wretched day of waiting had been as hard on Ives as it had been on any stockman, and so Ives wanted a showdown.

Loudon touched the rifle that rode in the scabbard at his knee. How many badlanders were cleaning rifles this morning? Odd how you got feeling akin to the enemy, seeing as how he was in the same fix as you.

Halfway between Long Nine and the Missouri, Frome brought them all to a stop. Frome huddled up with Singleton and Lathrop and Cottrell, and there was much talk. Finally a dozen men were called, one by one, Tex Corbin among them. More talk, and then the word came. Corbin was to take these men and head toward Castle Bend. They were to be a scouting party only, making no attack if they found that the badlanders had returned to the old wood yard. They were to send a fast rider to Craggy Point if need be.

Corbin and his crew struck off to the right, a knot of riders growing smaller with distance. Loudon wondered if he wished he'd been chosen to go with them. It didn't matter. What was the difference whether he triggered a gun or pulled on a rope or rode empty canyon trails, finding nothing? What there'd be of guilt would be a shared thing for all of them. That was something he'd read in Corbin's eyes this morning, and in Charley Fuller's try at grinning.

They rode on, and then the hours were behind, and the miles, and they were on the lip of the grade with the land sloping away and the river down there, snaky and dull, the willows bare, the town forlorn.

Here they held another consultation, Frome and Singleton and Lathrop and Cottrell bunching up again. The question seemed to be whether they should send somebody snooping ahead or just ride in, and Singleton's argument rose high. "Hell, they know we're coming. Let's ride."

Holding to a walk, they came down the slant, but the need in Loudon was to gallop. Here at the brink, he wanted to make the plunge and be done with the whole business, done with waiting. He saw the same need in the faces of others. Not a man spoke now.

No steamboat at the landing; no steamboat smoke hovering over the river. Loudon looked toward the landing and remembered being there with Clem Latcher while Joe McSween had ridden up this slant waving a last goodbye.

Then the cowboy army was off the slope and coming into the single street. He looked toward the livery stable and saw Ike Nicobar in the doorway, his eyes squinted down. He got the feeling that Ike was trying to tell them something, that Ike was sending up a silent shout. Nearly every door in town was closed and some windows were shuttered, and the silence hung heavy. In this hush, the jingle of bit chains and the creak of saddle leather made a kind of thunder. In Loudon, a feeling of tightness grew that was like an arm around him, shutting off his breath. The cowboy army moved slowly ahead till they were nearly abreast of the Assiniboine. *When?* Loudon thought. *When, damn it?*

A rifle spoke from the saloon's window; a bullet-stung horse bolted crazily.

At once the street became awhirl with milling, cursing riders. Horse crashed against horse. Frome was shouting above the bedlam. Badlander guns hammered from the Assiniboine, from the space between buildings, from roofs here and there. Cooler-headed cowboys took deliberate aim and answered gun with gun. Dust boiled up. A wounded horse cried its agony.

Loudon saw Shad Singleton tip from the saddle. *Dead!* he thought.

The hammer of his hand gun clicked on an empty shell. He tugged his Winchester from the saddle and hit the ground. Crouched behind his horse, he fired through the mist of dust. A loose horse drove at him, striking him, nearly knocking him down. He raced to the boardwalk and the protection of a water barrel before the Mercantile. From behind the barrel, he saw cowboys who had stood their ground now spurring for cover. The street emptied of riders, but gun-broke horses stood ground-tied by reins that had fallen. Shad Singleton wasn't the only dead man lying out there. The horses worried Loudon. Why the hell did men have to mix horses into their senseless doings?

Lead splintered the boardwalk and thudded into the Mercantile front behind him. He sent bullets at the window of the saloon. He shot systematically, wanting to get the man who had opened this fight. Damned if he wasn't freed now from whatever had held him frozen of mind all through the morning. *This is it,* he thought. Better than waiting and wondering. A bullet was the only answer to a bullet.

He jammed fresh cartridges into his rifle. How many men against them? He tried tallying the ambush guns and judged the badlanders to be about twenty. Hell, the cowboy army was half again as great as the force it now fought. Had Ives pinned his hopes on the ambush cutting down the odds before the stockmen could make their weight felt? Seemed so. And but for Frome, somewhere up the street shouting orders, Ives' strategy might have worked. Frome kept shouting for Looped L to move to the west end of the street where they had entered town. Rafter S and Boxed C he wanted at the east end. Long Nine was to skulk among the buildings. Loudon had to admire Frome for his generalship. He saw a man dart from beneath the overhang of the barber shop and around the corner. Charley Fuller. The townspeople were keeping behind doors and shutters. He worried about Ike.

A bullet smashed a stave out of the water barrel behind which he crouched. Another bullet drove into the barrel. Too hot here! He sprinted for the side of the mercantile; bullets pelted about him as he ran. He flung himself behind the wreckage of an old wagon box in the space between the Mercantile and the blacksmith shop. He rolled over, hugging his Winchester to him, and saw a rifleman atop the Assiniboine roof. The man savagely levered his gun and aimed, then levered again. That gun was either empty or broken. Loudon used his own rifle, and the man dropped from sight.

Got him, I think.

He kept looking for targets, his ears following the fight up and down the street. Guns hammered steadily; sometimes a voice lifted—"Long Nine!"—"Boxed C!"—as one man or another identified himself. Frome's notion was sure as hell working; his forces closed in like pincers, pushing the badlanders toward the center of town. Across the way a man sprinted for the Assiniboine. Loudon fired; the man went sprawling. The fellow got to his hands and knees and began to crawl, dragging his leg. A gun spoke somewhere down the street; the man fell forward and lay still. From the saloon, an angry roar rose.

Loudon heard boots crash down the dry stalks of weeds behind him. He swung, not knowing whether he would see friend or foe. Frome, Ab Cottrell, and Pete Wickes came up. Frome had lost his hat somewhere; dirt smeared one cheek. He looked at Loudon. "Hot here, Jess?"

A bullet sang close. Loudon got Frome by the arm and shouted, "Down!" He fell, dragging Frome behind the wagon box with him. The others dropped, too.

Frome rolled over on his side so that he could face Wickes. "Pete, work your way up the street. Find Buck Lathrop. Tell him to move a few of his men and cover the back door of the Assiniboine. We flush a man off a roof or out of a hole and he hits for that damned saloon."

Wickes backed away, came to a stand, and went

running. Frome got out his watch. "A half hour of this now," he said.

Loudon couldn't have told anybody if he had been here ten minutes or an hour. The ranch crews had worked so far down the street toward each other that friend stood a good chance of shooting friend.

Buck Lathrop showed up shortly, Pete Wickes with him, the two running a zigzag course till they fell to cover. Lathrop said, "We've got nearly all of them pinned over there." He nodded toward the Assiniboine.

"Then we'll fire the building," Frome said.

Ab Cottrell said, "My God, Frome, there's enough breeze to burn out the town!"

Frome's face fixed stonily. "We fire it anyway."

Cottrell, a wizened little man, shook his head. Buck Lathrop said, "Damn it, Frome, we're not a bunch of Indians!"

Frome turned to Pete Wickes. "Get down to the livery stable, Pete, and get some kind of rig. Load it with hay and set the hay on fire. You'll find men around there to help push it. I want it jammed tight to the Assiniboine wall."

Loudon said, "Frome, I'd think twice about that!"

But Wickes had begun crawling away. Frome said angrily, "There's no easy way to fight a war."

Spasmodic gunfire now, with the silence coming down and holding until Loudon ached for it to break. He felt that old numbness of mind coming back. Beside him, he heard Frome breathing deeply, evenly. In the next lull, the creak of wheels came plain. Loudon drew himself to a stand and stepped around the wagon box to where he could get a look down the street. A hay rack came moving along, the piled hay already ablaze. He judged that half a dozen men shoved the wagon, steering it by its tongue. Flames mounted and smoke billowed under the pushing of the breeze.

"Now!" Frome said.

Cottrell stood up. "Look, Frome! Look!"

A rifle barrel, with what appeared to be a bartender's apron hanging from it, showed outside the shattered window of the Assiniboine. Ives' voice reached from the depth of the building. "All right, we've had enough."

Frome got to his feet. "Come on out," he shouted.

Ives came first, staggering; his left arm hung limp, and there was dust in his hair. He held a gun in his hand.

"Drop it," Frome called.

Ives let the gun drop. Frome stepped forward and waved his arm to halt the burning hay rack. Ives stood in the street, sullen and defiant, yet looking crushed. More men came from the Assiniboine. They bunched together; Loudon counted over a dozen of them. He moved forward with Frome, and from the two ends of the street came Looped L men and Boxed C men and Singleton's crowd. Long Nine showed up from everywhere. All bore down upon Ives' group and surrounded it, and somebody lifted a coiled saddle rope and shook it above his head. This was a Rafter S man.

Frome said, "There's a clump of cottonwoods down by the river."

As a body, they began moving that way, crowding between two buildings and then bursting out upon the river bank. The badlanders were carried along in a tide of men. The Rafter S man with the rope had been cursing; but as the group moved into the trees, silence fell harder than before. Somebody came leading up horses. The trees spread their shadows over all, and the river made its mindless talk. Looking back,

Loudon saw a column of smoke rising from where the hay rack had been left standing in mid-street.

Frome said, "Ives first."

They got Ives' hands tied behind him and a loop swung over the branch of a cottonwood. Ives did not fight against them. They boosted Ives to a horse's back, and another of Singleton's men shouted, "Damn it, I get to handle the quirt!" Nobody disputed him.

Ives looked at Frome. "You might remember I didn't have to surrender. Not till we'd got a few more of you."

Frome said, "I owe you nothing."

One of the badlanders went down to his knees and began blubbering. "You're not going to hang me!" he cried. "You're not!" He beat at the knees of the men about him.

Ives looked down at him and said in a dead voice, "Bill, shut your damn' mouth."

For Loudon, the world had narrowed down to Ives' face. It was chalk-white, and a muscle in one cheek twitched. He wondered if Ives was really looking straight at him, or if it just seemed so. Their feud had been personal from that day in the Assiniboine; twice since, he had looked through the smoke of Ives' gun. Yet there was no satisfaction in this moment, no need but one that cried inside Loudon: *Go out brave, Jack! For God's sake don't break and start begging or fighting against this!* And he thought he knew from what that cry was fashioned: This was his enemy, and he wanted an enemy that was worthy. Or could it be that here at the hang-tree he liked Ives better than Frome?

The man with the quirt swung, and the horse leaped forward. Loudon could hear the rope jerk taut; he remembered Joe McSween. Then Ives was swinging, swinging . . .

Frome said, "Bring up another of them. Any one of them."

Finished now. Finished, with all the cottonwoods bearing fruit. Frome had said, "Leave them up for a day or so as a warning to others," but Lathrop had pointed out that there were no others; this was a clean sweep. Frome had nodded. Looped L, it was decided, would stay to do the burying. Rafter S and Boxed C would see to the cowboy dead and wounded. There was Singleton dead, and two of Looped L's men and one of Boxed C's, and half a dozen who needed wounds looked after. Some would have to be taken home in wagons.

All this they talked out, standing in the empty street of Craggy Point where the ruin of the hay rack smoldered, and again Frome did the generaling. Not once had that rock-like look left his face; Loudon wondered if it ever would. Then, at last, Frome stepped up to his saddle. He singled out men. "Grady," he said, "and you, Charley Fuller, come with me. Jess, you take the rest of our hands to Castle Bend and find Tex. If there's stock at that hideout, drive the stuff to Long Nine. And before you leave the wood camp, touch a match to cabin and corral and everything that stands."

Loudon nodded. He watched Frome ride out with Grady Jones and Charley Fuller, heading west. He found someone plucking at his elbow; it was Ike Nicobar. Ike said, "I couldn't call out to ye, Jess, when you rode in. That barn was lousy with 'em, and they'd have shot me down in a minute. Ye understand, Jess?"

"Sure. Forget it, Ike."

He walked away from Nicobar. He called together the others of Long Nine, and they rose to saddles and started along the street. On the edge of the boardwalk sat a cowboy, his head down between his knees. Loudon reined up close to him. It was Chip McVey, and he had been sick all over his boots.

"You all right, Chip?" Loudon asked.

"Lemme alone," Chip said. "God damn it, just lemme alone!"

18

The Ready Gun

STANDING IN HIS DOORWAY, CLEM LATCHER LOOKED OUT upon the Sunday hush of his ranch yard and felt calmness come upon him with a decision reached. He was free, and it felt good to be free. He breathed deep. Behind him, he could hear Addie stirring where she lay sprawled upon the bed, and the quietness of the room seemed to hold the whispering echo of the talking they had just done. No tears today. No harsh accusations, either; he had told her that he knew about Ives, that he had read Ives' face last night at Castle Bend and had his answer. She had neither confirmed nor denied; she had seemed not to care that he knew. She had let him do the talking, and he had said everything but the final thing.

Now, without looking at her, he spoke. "Addie, I am leaving you."

After a moment she asked, "When?"

"Today."

Did she sigh? And was it with regret or relief? He

wanted mightily to turn and read her eyes, but he knew he would see nothing in them but what she chose to let him see. So be it. His decision was still a good one; if she had protested, he might have wavered. As it was, he felt like a man done with a long sickness. Perhaps she wasn't protesting now because she, too, had hoped for a door to freedom. Probably she and Ives would go away together, if Ives lived through what cattledom planned for him. He found that he could think about them impersonally. He wished them happiness.

He said, "There is money in the Benton bank, Addie. You can still draw upon it at any time. If you want a divorce, I'll not fight it."

He stepped into the yard. He got his horse from the log stable and saddled. He would, he decided, not even bother with what extra clothes he had in the house. He wanted to take nothing with him from the life he was leaving. But when he rode into the sunlight of the yard, he heard his name called. She was standing in the doorway; she pushed back a lock of hair from her forehead. For a moment he was sure she was going to beckon to him, and he was panicked by the thought. Was his sense of freedom only an illusion after all?

"Yes, Addie?" he asked.

"Goodbye, Clem," she said. "I just wanted to say goodbye."

"Goodbye," he said.

"It's best this way, Clem. I guess we were a mistake for each other from the first."

"I guess so," he said.

"Try to think kindly of me, Clem."

"I shall try," he said without rancor, "never to think of you again. One way, or the other."

He rode out then, following the river downstream.

In his mind's eye, he kept seeing her standing in the doorway, and he forced his thoughts to other things. He would go to Craggy Point and stay there till a steamboat came downriver. He supposed he would go back East; he hadn't really thought about a destination. He would go back to the old place of his dead parents; he would go back to a monied comfort, to books. But he would go back defeated.

His full sense of loss came just like that, rising unbidden out of what he had supposed were safe thoughts. What kind of man was he, he asked himself fiercely, that everything he fashioned, even a decision of less than an hour ago, crumbled in his hands? What made him such a complete failure?

On the flats to his right stood stacks of hay. He had put up that hay with his own two hands. Well, that was a thing he had proved he could do. He began remembering all the places from which he had fled with Addie in the last ten years. What had he been looking for? Surely for more than a place where she could be free from her own restlessness. Surely he had been looking for something for himself as well. Whatever the quest, it had started before he'd known Addie. But whatever it was he sought, he had not found it in the other places, and he had not found it here.

He looked in the direction of the badlands. When he had first come here, he'd been both allured and repelled by the badlands. He had ridden the rocky desolation again and again. Seeking what? Himself, he supposed now. But still he'd been afraid, remembering always a thing he had found in his reading, the tale of Red Bird, the old Mandan chief, about how once the badlands had been meadow and forest, a rich hunting ground, until a fierce mountain tribe had dislodged the Indians who dwelt there. The medicine man of the dispossessed had then invoked the Great

Spirit on behalf of his people, and to the drumbeat of thunder the earth buckled and heaved until desolation claimed the hunting grounds. Thus the badlands had been born. And always since reading that account, he had seen them as a monument to wrath and been afraid. It was not superstition; he was too learned for that. But whenever he had ridden the badlands, he had sensed his own inadequacy.

That was it. Inadequacy. A mite of a man. He was inadequate for this frontier to which he had come, inadequate for the woman whose life had been bound up with his, inadequate for full forgetfulness of her in spite of his determination earlier today. He would go full circle back to the place whence he had started, and he would fall into the old groove of life, prowling the library that had been his father's. But all his days would be futile, for he would know his own inadequacy.

He thought this without self-pity. It was a cold appraisal, like reading what a printed page had to say about something that had happened to a man long gone.

He looked up to see riders coming along the river toward him. Three of them. Still deep in thought, he registered the presence of these men with his eyes only, and then he realized that one of the riders was Frome and the others were Grady Jones and Charley Fuller. Now what in the world had brought them here? Frome would be heading into the badlands today, a full force behind him, but this quiet river bank was a far piece from the badlands. He reined up and waited. When the riders were within ten feet, Frome drew to a stop, too, and so did the others. Grady Jones stared so hard that Latcher dropped his eyes.

Frome said, "Well, Clem—?"

A face like stone, Frome's. It made Latcher uncomfortable. To cover his embarrassment, he said, "I didn't expect to find you around here."

"Where do you think you're going, Clem?"

"To Craggy Point. I'm leaving this country."

Frome said, "So you're running!"

Latcher said without rancor, "I expect that's my business."

"Mine as well," Frome said. "We're making a clean-up today. To the last man. I'll not mince words, Clem. You've slow-elked beef for your own table."

Latcher said, "That's a lie."

Charley Fuller looked truly surprised. "Is that why we came this way? I don't believe it!"

Frome said, "Clem, you were seen sinking a cowhide weighted with rocks in the Missouri. I could dredge for that cowhide, but probably you cut the Long Nine brand out of it first. You know what that means."

Latcher shook his head. He felt caught up in a nightmare. "I tell you, you lie."

"Grady saw you sink that cowhide," Frome said. "I'm sorry, Clem."

Jones laid his hand on his saddle rope. "Do we jaw about it all day?" he demanded. "There's trees back a piece."

Something crowded Latcher's throat that was like laughter but strangled him as it rose. He got from his saddle and walked toward Frome and looked up at the man. He searched Frome's face for some sign of mercy. He shook his head. "You're making a terrible mistake."

"No mistake. I know what I'm doing."

The first inkling of understanding hit Latcher then. "So you rode into your badlands once too often."

Frome looked puzzled. "We weren't in the badlands. We found Ives' bunch at Craggy Point."

"You don't understand," Latcher said.

Jones said, "Get back on your horse, Latcher. We're done with talk."

For a moment Latcher could not speak, but in him was the drumming, ironic thought, *They can't kill me. They can't kill a dead man.* But instinct was in him, too, the instinct that makes the drowning kitten claw at the sack. That instinct gave him anger. And his anger fed on a full and terrible knowledge. Frome wanted him dead. And there was only one thing he'd ever had that any other man had wanted, and thus the truth stood clear.

"So it wasn't Ives after all," he said. "It was you."

He reached for Frome then. He got his hands on Frome's coat and tugged at the man, trying to pull him from his horse. He was beyond any reason, any desire but the desire to kill, and his anger tasted good in his throat. He had never before permitted himself full anger, but now he knew its power. It was the instrument to make him sufficient in this claw-and-fang world where he had been a stranger. He, too, could build a monument to wrath; he was his own drumbeat of thunder. He had found himself.

As through a haze he glimpsed Frome's scared look and Charley Fuller's dazed face. He heard a mighty oath rip out of Grady Jones, and he saw a gun come into Jones' hand and then tilt and spew. Something caught him hard in the chest, and he had only one thought then. He wanted to drag Frome down with him. He tried hard to hold to Frome as he went falling, falling. Then darkness came. . . .

By first starlight, Loudon came out of the badlands, feeling beat-out tired, feeling empty. Behind him the

Long Nine men hazed horses and cattle they'd found at Castle Bend; and with the crew was Tex Corbin's bunch, come upon deep in the canyons. Damn, but they'd nearly swapped bullets at meeting, Tex being edgy and not sure whether friend or foe was coming. Tex had found no one at Castle Bend, but that hadn't made him less hair-triggered.

Loudon looked back. No longer could he see the tower of smoke where the buildings of the old wood camp must still be blazing. He'd used the kerosene from every lamp and lantern he'd found. There'd be nothing standing come morning but a pile of ruins.

Loudon now rode in a shut-in world, though not so shut in as the canyons had been. No moon yet, and there wouldn't be much of one when it came. He supposed he should be itching to get to Long Nine. He hadn't eaten since morning, but he didn't feel for food now, nor even for a bed, though both hunger and tiredness had hold of him. He'd got that old numbness of mind back, and it stayed.

After a while he saw the lights of the ranch. Riding almost due west, he could also see the tiny light of the schoolhouse. A bad, bad business today. Elizabeth would know. Somebody would have stopped by and given her the word of what had happened at Craggy Point; maybe Frome himself. Still, he would go to Elizabeth. She'd be needing his shoulder to lean upon.

First, though, there was the recovered stock to be put behind fence and a report to be made to Frome. He, Jess Loudon, was the foreman with duties to see to. Foreman—? God, but that had meant something once, something strong and prideful, but even the word foreman now sounded senseless when he said it in his mind. Being foreman was a proud thing only when a man could be proud of his brand. Where, then, had he lost that pride? He remembered Frome speaking of firing the Assiniboine and Ab Cottrell protesting, and Frome saying, "We fire it anyway." Frome looking so rock-faced and uncaring of anything but his own wants.

Long Nine was looming up. Loudon dismounted and opened the gate of a fenced-off pasture and signaled for the men to spill the stock inside. There were other horses moving yonder in the darkness, the horses recovered from the first foray to Castle Bend, the ones that Frome hadn't got around to speaking about to their rightful owners.

Loudon rode on into the ranch yard with the men. Quite a few riders here, though not so many as last night; but still a good many Looped L and Rafter S and Boxed C men prowled about. Why the hell didn't they get on to their own ranches? The thing that had brought them all together was finished. Then Loudon guessed that some shared memory, some shared shame, was holding them close to each other.

Nearly every window in the ranch-house was lighted. A man would think Frome was throwing some kind of frolic. Or was it just that Frome didn't care for darkness tonight? Maybe Lathrop and Cottrell were there with him, and probably Grady Jones, who seemed to be more often in the house than in the bunkhouse lately. But no, Grady was here in the yard. He stood near the well, and Loudon felt the man's eyes on him, the stare so intent that he wondered if Grady had been waiting for him. But Grady didn't speak; he just stood watching.

The hell with him, Loudon thought.

The hell with Frome, too. Loudon climbed heavily back into his saddle. He didn't want to see Frome tonight, to make a report or for any other reason. Let Tex Corbin tell the boss whatever Frome needed to know. Loudon rode out of the yard and headed toward the schoolhouse.

He rode slowly. He had asked much of his horse today. He rode through the darkness, trying to keep his eyes on the schoolhouse, and after a time he came into the yard and was surprised to find himself here. Had he dozed awhile in the saddle? He stepped down and left the horse standing with reins trailing and moved forward and was astonished a second time. A small buckboard stood by the building, a team hitched to it. He went closer and found a leatherbound trunk in the buckboard. He knew that trunk; he had fetched it to Long Nine.

A splash of light fell upon the yard as Elizabeth opened the door.

"It's me," Loudon said.

"Jess, come in here!"

Her voice was taut, urgent. He stepped into the schoolhouse. She closed the door after him, and he looked at her in the lamplight. She looked as though she had been ill. He jerked his head in the direction of the wagon. "So you're leaving."

"I've just been waiting for you," she said. "If you hadn't come in another hour, I'd have gone to the ranch looking for you."

He said, "Last night there was something you had to know for sure about Frome. Now you're sure. Is that it?"

"Jess," she said, "they killed Clem today."

He got her by the shoulders and shook her fiercely, his own voice a roar in his ears. "What—?" he demanded.

Her words came with a rush. "Charley Fuller stopped by and told me. He was going to the ranch and get his stuff and ride away. He wasn't even going to wait to collect his pay. He was there with Frome and Grady Jones when it happened. They were going to hang Clem, but he put up a fight. Jones shot him down. Charley was scared—scared to death."

"Hang Clem? In the name of sense, why?"

"They said that Clem had butchered Long Nine beef. That made Clem a rustler, too. . . . Jess, you're hurting me."

He took his hands off her shoulders. He stood looking at his hands. God, but he was tired, so tired that he couldn't get sense out of what she said. Frome and Grady Jones and Charley Fuller . . . Now he knew where they had ridden after Craggy Point, but still this made no sense.

"Clem," he muttered. "Clem. He never stole anything in his life! That couldn't have been the reason." He began to shake.

"Charley told me," she said. "The last thing Clem said was, 'So it wasn't Ives after all. It was you.' That made no sense to Charley. It does to me. That's why I asked Charley to load my trunk at the ranch and bring it here."

"Yes," he said, "I savvy, too," and he was thinking, *Frome and Addie . . . Frome and Addie . . .* Ives put out of the way, and Clem to be next. Grady Jones, pampered lately and then taken along for the strong arm that might be needed. Charley Fuller taken, too, to give the whole thing a pretense of decency, with Charley a safe bet; he wasn't strong enough to stand up against the other two.

Then full anger came, and it was the first real thing he'd got hold of all day. It sloughed the weariness off him and brushed the numbness from his mind. He turned about and headed toward the door, but Elizabeth got hold of his arm.

"No, Jess!" she cried. "Not that way. Don't you see why I've waited for you? It's you I'm worried about!

Frome took one step today, so now he'll have to take another. Whom will he fear? What one man would come after him for Clem?"

"Me," he said, and wrenched free of her.

"Jess, don't do it his way! He's got to pay for what he's done, kin or not. But we'll go to Miles City. We'll go to the Stockgrowers' Association and make a charge."

"No!" he said.

He got through the door. He heard her call, but he pulled the door shut behind him. For a moment he stood in the darkness; he was no longer shaking; his anger was a terrible, cold calmness. He peered, looking for his horse. He took a step, and something stiffened the hairs at the back of his neck. Not ten feet away was the motionless shape of a man. He knew that man because Grady Jones, who'd been waiting at Long Nine, was waiting again. Elizabeth had guessed right about the fear that would now be Frome's and the necessity that would have grown out of that fear.

Once earlier today the gun of Grady Jones had been ready. It would be ready now. Knowing this, Loudon made a try for his own gun. He saw the red smear of flame and heard the crash of Jones' gun. Or was the roar in his own head? He reached out blindly. He grasped at air, and grasping, fell.

19

Steamboat on the River

THERE WAS A THING TO BE GOT HOLD OF, BUT IT WAS JUST beyond reach, just beyond the edge of his mind. Sometimes he was greatly troubled and searched through endless caverns of darkness. Other times he was a man drifting on an easy river; and he had only to lie back then, calm in the surety that he would find what it was that eluded him. He kept saying his name, *Jess Loudon—Jess Loudon,* over and over to himself, wanting to hold onto that familiar sound. The worst times were when there was hardness under him, a bucking, heaving hardness that he identified as a wagon, but he couldn't be sure whether the rough riding was something he was experiencing or something he was remembering.

After a long while it came to him that it was a name he hunted. If he could only lay hold of that name, he could dally around it and make fast. He kept searching through the pain, the sharp, hot pain. He tried batting at rough hands and the burn of a blade, but he couldn't lift his arms. He made out a face dimly, and he thought, *Grady Jones!* Now he'd found the name, and anger went through him, sharp and hot as the blade. He tried to claw at the whiskers hovering over him. Whiskers—? Grady Jones didn't have whiskers. Jones wasn't here for him to get hold of. But he'd found more than the name; he knew now what it was he'd hunted through the darkness. A notion. He had to kill Grady Jones; yes, and Peter Frome. He hugged the notion to him and fell into a deep sleep.

He awoke to a morning. He lay staring at high rafters and knew he was in a barn. He put out a hand and found that he lay upon a blanket and was bedded in hay. His left shoulder seemed heavy. He could see the dust that swirled in the shafting light from a window beyond his vision. He felt a hand upon his forehead and heard Elizabeth say, "No fever." He turned his head. She was sitting beside him, her legs curled under her in the hay. She looked thin.

He wanted to talk, but it seemed too great an effort. He lay still and listened and began to sort out sounds. Street sounds—the creak of buggy wheels, the beat of boots on planking, the shouted good morning of one man to another. Finally he asked, "Craggy Point?"

"You're in the loft of Ike's livery stable," Elizabeth said. "Do you think you could eat?"

"I don't know," he said; but he heard the words only faintly. He guessed he was falling asleep again . . .

He opened his eyes to dusk, the soft dusk of an early evening, and almost at once he heard a rustling movement in the hay and saw Elizabeth's face bent over him. "Here," she said. She gave him water. Some of it ran down his chin. He raised his right hand to wipe off his chin; he felt the heavy stubble on his cheeks and jaw. He sighed and lay back upon the blanket, and then he was troubled by something he had to grope for again.

"Clem," he said at last. "I want to go to Clem's funeral."

"That was here in Craggy Point," she said. "The day before yesterday."

He was disappointed and a little puzzled. He had, he guessed, been far out and away for a long while. He tried remembering everything that might give him the key to time. He worked backwards in his mind to that waiting figure in the schoolhouse yard and the crash of the gun and his falling. He could remember a scream, too—that must have been Elizabeth rushing out into the yard. After that, there had been the beat of boots as Jones had run.

"You got me into the wagon," he decided.

"You were able to help yourself some," she said. "When I got you on your feet, you were still out from shock. I don't know yet how we managed. I was in a panic, thinking that he'd come back, but I guess he thought he'd left you dead. I wanted to race the team to town, but I didn't dare. I'd put the best bandage on you I could fix in a hurry, but I was afraid you'd die on the road."

The ladder to this loft creaked, and he saw Elizabeth's face stiffen and fear flicker in her eyes. He struggled, trying to prop himself on an elbow. Ike Nicobar came into his range of vision and peered from behind his whiskers. "Ye ready for a bait o' grub, Jess?"

"I could eat," he said.

"Some soup," Ike said. "That will start the sap runnin' in ye again."

Loudon remembered the burning blade. "You got the bullet out of me, Ike?"

"With an old skinnin' knife. Plugged up the hole afterwards with a wad of Climax and a hunk o' horse blanket."

Elizabeth said, "I couldn't think of anywhere to bring you but to Ike." Her voice shook. "Once I was here, I wanted to ride to Benton and get a doctor. Too far, Ike said. Besides, he was afraid that fetching a doctor might give away where you were hidden. He said Jones would come looking again, sooner or later, just to make sure. That very night Ike drove the wagon half-way back to Long Nine and then unharnessed the team and turned it loose. He's got your horse hidden out."

Loudon said, "Thanks, Ike," but the old man was gone. Queer that he hadn't heard Ike leave. Shortly Ike came back carrying a steaming pot of broth. Loudon tried sitting up, but he couldn't make it. Elizabeth ladled the soup into him. After that, he slept again.

He awoke to a new morning and to a feeling of strangeness, a feeling that all was not well. Elizabeth wasn't beside him. He managed to push himself up, and he saw her then. She was out on the bare center of the floor, stretched there full length, peering through a knot hole into the barn area below. She held a gun. He recognized the gun. It wasn't the one he'd given her to keep at the schoolhouse; it was his own. He strained his ears, trying to make out if Ike was talking to anyone below. He could hear nothing but the movement of horses in the stalls. After a while Elizabeth lifted herself from the floor and turned and saw him staring.

"Grady Jones," she said.

He tried getting to his feet. He did not have the strength for it. He became angry at his own weakness; he felt like cussing or crying, or both. Elizabeth came and gently pressed him back against the blankets. He lay still.

Soon Ike came to the loft. Elizabeth talked to the old man, and Ike disappeared. It must have been over an hour before he came back and made a whispered report to Elizabeth and was gone again.

Loudon asked irritably, "What the hell is going on?"

"Grady's left town," Elizabeth said. "He prowled around most of the morning, not asking questions, but just looking, but he's gone now. Back toward Long Nine, Ike says."

He was sick from anger. He lay back fighting the fury, knowing that he had no strength to waste on fury. Not yet. Finally he slept. He was to doze and wake through the next several days. Usually Elizabeth was beside him when he awoke; sometimes she wasn't. From Ike he learned that she had taken a room at the hotel. If anyone came to her from Long Nine, she would deny all knowledge of Loudon.

He worried about her then, thinking that Jones might come to her hotel room. Or Frome. He was glad she had his gun. He got sickest whenever he thought of Frome. He remembered how once he'd wondered whether he stood taller than Frome. Hell, flat on his back he stood taller! He got impatient whenever Elizabeth was gone; he got so he could tell the creak of the ladder when her weight was on it.

He owed his life to her courage and to her good sense in thinking of Ike and bringing him here. He thought of that many times.

He found himself going over and over what had happened just before he'd been stripped of his strength. He remembered the cowboy army moving upon this town; he remembered the fight and the hangings afterwards and how he had wanted Jack Ives to go out brave. But mostly he remembered going to the schoolhouse that night and hearing of Clem's death and then stepping into the yard and into disaster.

Damn, but he still couldn't quite grab onto the truth that Clem was dead, yet he knew it was so. Dead and buried. Well, he would square up for Clem. He'd known that in unconsciousness and in pain; he knew it more clearly with each passing day. But he'd have to have strength, and so he rested and ate the food Ike and Elizabeth fetched and put his effort into getting back his strength. He was cunning about this, knowing that Ike and Elizabeth would be alarmed if they discovered the true core of his eagerness.

Sometimes, when Elizabeth was gone to the hotel and he was sure that Ike was out of the barn, he tried walking. At the first attempt he fell, but on another day he managed a few tottering steps, and on the next day he was able to get across the loft and back to his blanket. He was slow about this; it was almost as though he had to learn how to walk all over again. But he slept soundly afterwards and was as pleased as a child with the achievement. The next day he walked the loft several times.

The morning after that, a steamboat whistle awakened him.

He was faintly surprised. He hadn't supposed there'd be another boat this season. Was it still October? He tried to piece the days together, but there were gaps, and there were separate things he could remember but couldn't be sure whether they'd happened on the same day or on different days. He guessed it was two or three days over a week since he'd been brought here, and that would make it just about the last week in October. Pretty late. That steamboat captain might find himself frozen in some morning.

Ike was puttering around below; he could hear the old man's shovel scrape as Ike cleaned off the barn runway. Then Ike was talking to someone, and the other man was talking, too; and something cold touched Loudon's skin.

The second voice was Frome's.

Loudon sat bolt upright on the blanket. He risked noise then, moving to the knot hole Elizabeth had used. He peered, but he couldn't see either man. He could hear the talk more clearly, though. Frome was turning a horse and buggy over to Ike. Something about one of the Long Nine hands picking up the rig later.

Both men moved out of the barn. Loudon's first panicky thought was that Frome was here to look for Elizabeth, but he knew better when he considered that Frome was leaving the buggy. He looked about him. All these days he'd been dressed except for his boots and belt. He got into his boots and found his hat and shook the hay from it. He looked for his gun and then remembered that Elizabeth had it. He went to the ladder and began to descend.

He was slow about this, for he felt mighty light-headed, yet all the while the urge in him was to hurry. He had guessed by now what had fetched Frome to the Point. Frome was going aboard that steamboat; he was going beyond reach. The job was to get him before he got away. Loudon lowered himself to the barn floor. Horses switched their tails in the stalls, but no one was in sight. Ike would be wheeling the buggy around to the wagon yard. Loudon thought of a gun. He wondered if he should rummage for one of Ike's. No time, damn it.

He walked out to the street. Sunlight here and a clear sky overhead; it would be warm this afternoon, though just now the air was crisp. He looked up the street and down it and saw a few townspeople. He guessed he was a sight with hay clinging to his clothes and the bulge of a bandage thrusting at his shirt over his left shoulder and whiskers on him almost as long as Ike's. The hell with that!

He began walking toward the landing and saw a cluster of men there, and beyond them the boat. He made out the name painted on the pilothouse, *Argus.* Another ungainly cut-down mountain boat, sister to the *Prairie Belle,* with steam up and the black smoke belching from her twin stacks. Loudon tried hurrying faster. Seemed he was walking on air, and he shook his head trying to get the dizziness from it. If he could just get a real hold of himself! The crowd was thinning out on the landing; he saw a few boxes that had been unloaded from Fort Benton. No sign of Frome. The deck hands were casting off lines. Up above, the pilot was raising his hand to a signal cord.

He forced himself to a ragged run. He got to the wharf and pushed his way among men and reached the plank that crossed over to the main deck where cargo was piled. The paddle wheel was beginning to slosh. He gained the deck, and a roustabout came up to him and said, "Better pile off unless you figure to go along. We're not wasting any more time here."

Loudon put his hand on the man's chest and pushed him aside. He made his way unevenly toward a companionway and climbed it to the boiler deck. Again dizziness swept him, and he stood holding hard to a stanchion, trying to keep from falling. Beneath him the planking of the boat trembled, and he looked toward the landing and saw an expanse of water. That brown strip grew as he watched. The steamboat was already out in the current. Well, he could always get off at the first wood camp. He'd get hold of a horse somewhere and get back to Craggy Point. He couldn't worry about things like that now.

Another roustabout came along. He looked at Loudon in a surprised way. Loudon peered at the man. "Frome?" he asked. "Where's Frome?"

"Just stowed his trunk for him," the roustabout said. "Third cabin down on this side."

Loudon lurched along. Hard to walk here on this throbbing deck, though he couldn't recall that he'd ever had trouble on any other steamboat. Damn, but he was weak. Didn't have a thing to hold onto any more but a notion. He reached the third door. He had counted very carefully. He put out a hand and braced himself against the door jamb. He shook his head again, clearing it. Then he threw his weight against the door and felt it give under him, and he half-fell into the cabin.

20

Frome

ON THIS THE EVE OF HIS DEPARTURE, PETER FROME prowled the Long Nine ranch-house lighting lamps. In the midst of this activity he caught himself and frowned. Come to think about it, lamplighting had got to be a habit this past week or so. Why, he wondered. No taint of cowardice in it, he was sure; it just gave him something to do in this big, empty house. More than one night, though, he had left a lamp burning by his bedside and found the pale flame still flickering at dawn. "You want to set the damn' house afire?" Grady Jones had asked.

Thank heavens Grady wasn't around tonight. He had got mighty tired of Jones. The man was still out trying to make sure whether Jess Loudon was alive or dead, on this range or skipped. Jones hadn't found any trace of Loudon in Craggy Point the other day, and he'd showed back at the ranch to report and have something to eat and go hunting again. The blundering fool! Why had he bolted when Elizabeth had come running from the schoolhouse screaming? Why hadn't he stayed to learn if it was a live man or a dead one Elizabeth had got into the wagon and hauled away? Queer about that wagon being left standing in the middle of nowhere. Blood on the boards, but nothing much else to tell any kind of story.

And Elizabeth—? She'd headed back to Ohio, likely. Gone home hating him. Nothing he could do about that. He supposed he was well rid of her. Blind and unreasonable as her father before her, she was.

He roamed the house. He went into the kitchen and picked up the coffee pot from the stove but decided he wanted no coffee. He opened the back door and looked toward the lighted bunkhouse, then closed the door. He moved back into the parlor and took a book from a shelf and flipped the pages. He laid the book aside. Finally he went into his bedroom and sat upon the edge of the bed and began tugging at his boots.

He'd have to rise early tomorrow. Let's see, when was that steamboat scheduled to reach Craggy Point? He'd written down the time on the back of an old envelope after Tex Corbin had come home from Fort Benton, where he'd checked with the captain of the *Argus*. Last boat of the season, Tex had reported. There was skim ice on the water pails these mornings.

High time he was making the St. Louis trip that he'd promised himself earlier in the fall. Mostly the rustler trouble had stood in his way. He'd damn' well put that behind him, though. Now he could be a rancher again, going about his business. Better not forget to put his ledgers into the trunk. He padded in his stocking feet into the office and got the ledgers. He ran his hands over the buckram covers. He had some figures to make the eyes of those St. Louis bankers pop.

He got shed of his clothes and climbed into bed. Maybe a few sour faces would have the stiffness worked out of them by the time he returned upriver next spring. What the hell was the matter with everybody that they froze up whenever he came near? Was it because he hadn't gone to Clem Latcher's funeral? He'd decided that to go would be in very bad taste indeed, but he'd sent Grady Jones to scout the affair. Jones had reported that both Ab Cottrell and Buck Lathrop were there. Addie Latcher, he said, had stood stiff as a rock all through the funeral, not crying or carrying on a bit.

The very next day Rafter S had held Shad Singleton's funeral on the ranch; and he, Peter Frome, had gone and found nearly everybody from the range gathered. He had paid his respects to Mrs. Singleton and the three Singleton children and stood silent and sober while a circuit-riding preacher had said the words and Shad Singleton had been lowered into the earth. Afterwards he had sought out Buck Lathrop and extended his hand and said, "A black day for all of us, Buck." But Lathrop hadn't seemed to see his hand. Perhaps Buck had just been in a daze. He'd turned away from Lathrop and gone looking for Ab Cottrell; but Ab, climbing into his buckboard, hadn't appeared to hear when Frome had called his name across the heads of the crowd.

A fine pair of friends! Both Lathrop and Cottrell—yes, and Singleton, too—had come around early last summer, belly-aching about their rustling losses and talking big about what they were going to do; but none had made the first move. They'd left that to Peter Frome. It was he who'd gone to Miles City and got the tacit blessing of the Stockgrowers' Association and then led the first foray into the badlands. Without him, the others would still be sitting on their thumbs. But with the job done, they could turn their faces from him because he'd been a little rough. What kind of picnic had they thought it was going to be, anyway?

His own crew was none too friendly, for that matter. The day after the Craggy Point clean-up, he had made Grady Jones foreman, telling the boys in the bunkhouse only that Jess Loudon had moved on. They hadn't raised any question about Jess' being missing, any more than they were asking why Charley Fuller had ridden away. He was sure that not one of them knew about Grady Jones' trailing Jess to the schoolhouse and opening up on him, so it wasn't suspicion that was making the crew glum. And with Grady gone most of this past week, Frome had appointed Tex Corbin strawboss. Long Nine would be starting its roundup tomorrow. Tex was popular with the boys, and he'd supposed that Tex's promotion would please them; but any time he walked into the bunkhouse, the silence came down so thick he could slice it.

He'd do some weeding out when he got back from St. Louis, he promised himself. He didn't have to take sour looks from men who drew their pay from him.

He glanced at the lamp burning on the stand beside the bed. He reached out to extinguish it, but he compromised by turning down the wick. The trouble was that faces sometimes came crowding at him in full darkness, the faces of Jack Ives and those others at Craggy Point. But mostly he saw Clem Latcher.

Damn it all, he'd had a right to put Clem under. He remembered that session in the kitchen Saturday before last when he'd sat with Grady Jones, and Grady had made some remark about not trusting Clem too much. Jones had said that no small rancher ever ate his own beef. Then Clem had come stumbling in from the badlands to report that Ives was defiant about the ultimatum. Jones had studied Clem all the while. When Clem had left, Jones asked, "What would you say if I could prove Latcher's been slow-elking Long Nine beef?"

"I wouldn't believe it."

"Even if I told you I saw him sinking a cowhide in the Missouri?"

"Damn it, Grady, the man's got no need to steal!"

Jones shrugged. "Have it your way."

After he had got to bed that night, he thought about what Jones had said. It had been late, for Shad Singleton had showed up an hour after Latcher made his report, and they'd sat up together another hour making war plans. Peter Frome had had too much on his mind to be bothered about Jones' accusation. But maybe there *was* something to that sunken cowhide business. Jones had as good as said that Latcher should be hunted down and included in the clean-up.

No reason for Grady Jones to want Clem Latcher dead. Quite the contrary. Jones had a hold on Peter Frome only because Jones knew about that first midnight ride to the river ranch when Clem had been far away. With Clem dead, Peter Frome could ride openly; moreover, he'd no longer have to abide the insolence of Grady Jones. Jones was shrewd enough to know that, so Jones wouldn't be foolishly throwing away an ace. Of that Frome had been sure.

But the next day he had looked upon Jack Ives dead and known then what he was going to do next. He had named Grady Jones and Charley Fuller to go with him, and they had headed for Latcher's and met Latcher on the way.

The hell of it was, he hadn't freed himself from Jones with Latcher's death. He was more in Jones' power than ever before. He hadn't ordered Jones to go gunning for Jess Loudon, but when Jones had told him of the bungled attempt afterwards, he had known that Loudon's death was necessary, for the protection of his own skin as well as Jones'. He and Jones were tied together tighter than ever. How had Jones been so devilishly clever? How had Jones been sure, when he'd talked against Clem, that throwing away one ace would give him another, stronger one?

Frome turned over in bed. Jones had yet to learn who the smart man was. Once on the steamboat Peter Frome would write a letter to the federal marshal in Helena. He would tell him that Clem Latcher had died through no order of his, and that there was a man named Charley Fuller who could prove it. He would ask the marshal to look through his list of wanted men for one who met the description of Grady Jones.

He closed his eyes. He was tired of chasing such thoughts around. He was tired of Long Nine and this range with its threat of winter coming. He'd be on his way in the morning; he would gain for himself time to forget and to have others forget, and then, in the spring, he would come back . . .

He awoke feeling tired and depressed; the pale flame still burned beside his bed. He turned up the lamp, for this was the darkness before dawn, gray and cold. He got dressed and groped to the kitchen, and Sam came in and made him breakfast. When he came out to the yard, dawn was just beginning to color the east, over the badlands. Tex Corbin had got his trunk into the buggy and a horse hitched up. The man stood by.

Corbin asked, "You want I should ride in with you and fetch the rig back?"

Frome said, "No need. I'll leave it at the livery, and you can have somebody pick it up later."

"Okay," Corbin said.

Frome rose to the seat and unwrapped the reins from around the whipstock. Corbin was already fading back in the direction of the bunkhouse. No goodbye; no good wishes for a happy trip; nothing.

Frome drove out.

He came past the schoolhouse in the first flush of real light. No smoke showing, no children coming. He'd have to see about another teacher; perhaps he could engage one in St. Louis. Now that the rustler trouble was taken care of, other things could go forward. He remembered his old dream of schools and churches and towns; he tried to hark up his old enthusiasm. He guessed he was tired this morning.

At a fork of the road where he might have gone on directly toward Craggy Point, he veered to the left, and by mid-morning he was wheeling down the slant to Latcher's place.

He had not planned this until he reached the fork. He had seldom thought of Addie this past week, and even now he wasn't sure how he felt about her. A part of him cried that he did not want to see her again, that having fully attained her, he no longer wanted her. But still the old pull drew him. She, too, would need to get away, to look upon new faces and new vistas for a while. He could engage a cabin for her on the boat, being careful about this so that their connection would not be obvious. They could be circumspect, even make a pretense of indifference all the way to St. Louis, if need be; and after that the city could swallow them. Thinking this, his hands began to tremble.

The place looked almost as deserted as the schoolhouse when he wheeled into the yard, but a wisp of smoke rose from the chimney. He stepped down from the buggy and knocked upon the door, but there was no answer. He stood frowning. He called her name. A sense of alarm seized him, and he went around a corner of the house and reached a window. He shielded his eyes with cupped hands and peered inside. She lay upon the bed, fully clothed. She had heard him at the window, for she was looking his way. She shook her head. Her face was empty of any real emotion. She might have been dead but for her eyes; they stared at him and through him and beyond him.

"Addie!" he called.

She shook her head again. She turned over on the bed, putting her back to him.

Anger smote him; he had had enough of people who put their backs to him one way or another. He went around to the door and shook the handle, but the door was barred inside. He looked toward the buggy. He'd wasted time and lengthened the miles to Craggy Point by taking this fork of the road. He got back into the buggy and lashed the horse and fled along the river bank in the direction of the settlement. Soon he came to the spot where he and Grady and Charley Fuller had met Clem Latcher. He wondered then if Addie's abandonment of him had come from what had happened to Clem or from what had happened to Jack Ives. He couldn't know, and yet he did know; it was because of Clem.

He drove on. The steamboat was at the landing when he sighted town. He wheeled the buggy onto the wharf and had a roustabout remove his trunk, and then he drove on to the livery stable. He did not linger long, merely telling old Nicobar what to do. The roustabout had said something about their casting off at once. He went hurrying back to the landing and up the plank. He climbed a companionway. A deck hand told him which cabin had been assigned to him. He got into the cabin and closed the door and sank down upon a chair. He felt as though he'd been running a long time.

Presently he heard the whistle scream and the boat tremble. A sense of extreme satisfaction swept over him; he was on his way; he was on his way! He thought with amazement, *This is how a fugitive feels,* and he wondered from whom he had been running. Buck Lathrop and Ab Cottrell? Tex Corbin and all the glum crew? Addie? What were they, really, in his scheme of things? Futile, insignificant folk, earth bound and worthy only of contempt.

His old surety came back to him; he was just making a beginning! He thought of his Ohio boyhood, and of the gold camps, and of the long search across the land for graze to his liking. He thought of what he had so far reared on the naked prairie. By the Lord, all his doings had been only first steps on a long, long journey; all the rest lay ahead, the full realization of his powers, the full fruits of achievement.

Then the door burst open and a man lurched into the cabin.

Frome was on his feet before he recognized him, for Jess Loudon, looking tattered and hard used, a thick stubble on his face, wasn't the man he had known. Loudon seemed more dead than alive; he had to put out a hand and brace himself against the wall, but he said in a distinct voice, "Frome, I've come here to kill you."

Something crumpled inside Frome then, and pure terror rose up and caught him. His mind was a riot of scattered thoughts. He wanted to babble that there need be no trouble, that Jess Loudon could have back the foremanship, or a partnership, or anything he wanted. He tried to scream out that he was guiltless, that it was Grady Jones who'd killed Clem Latcher. He wanted to beg for mercy; he wanted to threaten. And now he knew what had really haunted his nights and why today he had been running; now he knew whom he had feared and fled, for Jess Loudon was here.

In panic he rushed at Loudon and threw his great bulk against him, knocking him down. Loudon clutched at his knees and nearly brought him to the floor. He wrenched free of Loudon and got through the door and stumbled out upon the deck. He looked over his shoulder and saw Loudon scrambling to his feet. There were roustabouts here on the deck, and he glimpsed the blue and brass of an officer's uniform. He screamed an appeal to these men, but he could not wait for them to help, and he began running toward the end of the deck. Loudon, out of the cabin, was coming after him.

Frome's breath was a rasp in his throat and a flame in his chest. He glimpsed water and the not-too-distant shore line and the lifting badlands beyond. He neared the stern and careened against the rail and was sure that he felt Loudon's hand upon his collar; but when he glanced back wildly, Loudon was still a good distance behind. He stared at Loudon; he turned and stared into the swirling river below. Then he made his choice and went over the rail in a clumsy dive.

Thunder was everywhere. Thunder swirled around him and closed in and seemed to have hands that seized him. He was choking and gasping in the water, and above him rose a great wall, the paddle wheel. He fought its pull and heard his own scream in his ears, and he flailed wildly and felt himself drawn into the heart of the thunder.

21

The Badlands

A LOT OF PEOPLE COMING AND GOING AT LONG NINE THESE days. Loudon, who daily sunned himself on the bench beside the bunkhouse, had watched buggies and buckboards and saddle horses swing in and out of the yard. He'd lost count of how many men had climbed the ranch-house steps, hat in hand, looking properly solemn. Buck Lathrop and Ab Cottrell had been here, and a good many other ranchers. Politicians from Helena had showed up to pay their respects, and men from the Stockgrowers' Association at Miles. And just this morning there had been a couple of lawyers with muttonchop side-whiskers and heavy leather cases who'd stayed closeted with Elizabeth for an hour or more.

Mighty lonesome in the yard, though. Only one of the dogs in sight, and a couple of horses in a corral. The crew was out on fall roundup, and Loudon wished he was with them. In the first days after his return he had liked lazing around, soaking up the thin fall sunshine or sleeping as late as he pleased; but now that he felt considerably stronger, he ached to be about and doing. The doctor from Benton, looking in on him yesterday, had as good as said he was fit for anything.

That doctor had been a bit worried the first day he'd come to Long Nine to look at Jess Loudon's wound. The wound had got torn open in the tussle he'd had in the steamboat cabin with Frome; and although the steamboat men had patched him up before they'd set him ashore at the first wood camp, they hadn't the savvy in their fingers that Ike Nicobar had. They'd done the best they could, at that. And they hadn't held against him what had happened to Frome. The captain himself had been one of those on the boiler deck when Frome had gone over the rail; he'd seen that Loudon hadn't been within lariat length of Frome at the time.

"If you need me to testify about what happened," he'd said to Loudon at parting, "I'll be back in the spring."

God, but it could all come back to Loudon any time! Sitting here in the sunlight, with the hush of the yard around him, he didn't even need to close his eyes to see Frome there against the steamboat rail, making up his mind and then making the leap. Seemed as though the steamboat shuddered after that, the paddle wheel missing a beat or two. He remembered throwing up his hands before his face, even though Frome had been beyond his sight; he'd wanted to shut out what his mind was seeing. And he'd thought of Joe McSween drunk and walking the rail, flapping his arms and crowing like a rooster, and how he and Ike Nicobar had worried about Joe's maybe going overboard and getting caught in the wheel.

He'd twitched in his sleep, thinking about Frome, the night he'd spent at the wood camp. The wood-hawk had gone out to search the river bank for Frome's body, but it hadn't come up. Loudon had wondered if it ever would; the Big Muddy had held tight to a lot of dead men.

It had taken him most of the next day to get back to Craggy Point; the only horse he'd been able to borrow had been a bony nag, and the trail had been rough. His torn shoulder had hurt like hell. Ike had given him Frome's buggy when he'd got to town, and Elizabeth had driven him home. They hadn't said much to each other on that ride. He had told Elizabeth about what had happened to Frome, making it as gentle as he could.

After a long hush, lasting a good mile or two, Elizabeth had said in a dead voice, "We were close kin, you know. Once he said that everything he built would belong to me. Including such honor as he could bring to his name." She shuddered. "What kind of heritage have I really got, Jess?"

He thought about this, wanting the answer to be something she could always lean on. "He was one person," he said at last. "You are another."

Then they had come home. He had moved his fixings from the house to the bunkhouse in spite of Elizabeth's protest that he should keep the foreman's room in the house till he got completely well. With the crew out on the range, he pretty much had the bunkhouse to himself anyway. He was foreman again, he supposed, though Tex Corbin was ramrodding the roundup. It didn't matter. Ambitious he'd been, but he'd seen where ambition had taken Frome. He had quite another thing on his mind now. He had formed a notion in the fever and pain of the first bullet shock, and he had not lost sight of that notion even though half the chore he'd set for himself was now done.

Sitting here, he let his thinking build and was

suddenly done with patience. Today was as good a day as any. He got up and walked to the corral and found his steps steady enough. He shook out a ketch-rope and laid a loop on his own gelding and got the saddle and bridle on. Good! He'd never been better on his best day. He went to the bunkhouse and got the gun Elizabeth had given back to him. He led out the horse and mounted and rode half across the yard, and then, like another time, he went to the blacksmith shop and rummaged around till he found a short-handled shovel.

Elizabeth was waiting in the yard when he came out. She was wearing that high-collared dress she'd worn on the *Prairie Belle* the day she arrived. It was her best dress, he guessed, and she wore it often lately, with so much company coming and going.

He said, "Morning, Elizabeth," and tied the shovel to his saddle.

"You're going after Grady Jones," she said.

He nodded. "Either he's scouted the place and seen that I'm back, or else he's heard. He'll not show up here. If he's still on this range, he's out in the badlands."

"Let him stay there, Jess."

"No," he said.

"Will nothing I can say show you how wrong you are?"

He didn't reply. He led the horse across the yard to the cook-shack and had Sam fix him up a sack of grub and a water bag. With these tied to the saddle, too, he mounted and rode out. When he looked back, Elizabeth was still standing in the yard, the wind whipping at her skirts. He raised his hand to her.

Such was the way he began his search.

He got into the badlands that afternoon and headed straight for Castle Bend. He reached the place late in the afternoon and found it deserted; the charred ruins of cabin and corral looked bleak in the sunlight. The river made its talk and the cliffs loomed high, and the clip-clop of his horse's hoofs raised echoes that flung about till they were lost. He sat his saddle for a while. Nothing here. Nothing but memories of a night of violence and a day when the flames had risen. He was glad to be on his way again.

He began prowling, threading canyon after canyon. He slept where darkness overtook him, and he rose with the sun and was into the saddle again. One day became like another, full of restless moving. In the nights, he kept his campfires small or made none, the silence and the rocks all around him. He was soon running low on grub, and he began to ration himself, riding hungry for long hours. He thought of the ranch, where more food could be got; he thought of Craggy Point, but still his trail took him farther from those places. Nothing showed that he could knock over with his gun and turn into meat. At last he came out on the eastern side of the badlands, and that day he found a sheep camp. He asked the sheepherder about Grady Jones.

"Ain't seen nobody," the sheepherder said.

He got grub from the man and turned back into the badlands. Jones was bound to be holed up somewhere, at least till he could be sure that Frome was really dead. He began a zigzag crossing, prowling here and there, following canyons that as often as not led to dead ends, pondering over sign, the clear mark of a horse's hoofprint in a sandy stretch the wind hadn't touched, a pile of horse droppings no more than a week old, the charred sticks where a campfire had once burned. An empty tin can was for him a book to be read, but always the pages were blank.

Yet the feeling was growing on him that Jones was

near, very near. Once he caught a whisk of motion atop a distant ridge, and after that he was extra careful where he camped, and he slept light and fitfully.

By night he lay in his blankets and stared up at the cold, clear stars. By day he rode through a chilliness that increased until he wished he had brought a warmer coat. The sky had become overcast; he remembered the sunshine of a week before, remembered it longingly. But still he rode on. He tried counting up the days he'd been on this search. The roundup would be over, and Long Nine would be pushing beef to Miles City and the waiting cars. He was suddenly homesick to be with Tex and Pete Wickes and Skinny Egan and the others; he could almost smell the dust of the trail. The prettiest thing he could have heard just then would have been the bawling of a cow.

And that night he built a big fire. He had come upon a seep spring, and brush grew near it, and he kept heaping on brush till the flames soared high. He took off his gun belt and laid it upon a rock so that the holster was in shadow but the belt loops showed. His gun he put close beside him, under the nearly-empty grubsack.

He had reached a decision; it had come suddenly, and he was free from what had driven him across all the days since Elizabeth had first told him that Clem Latcher was dead. Trouble was, he had thought only of Clem dead, when he should have remembered Clem alive. He should have remembered what Clem had said about each man's badlands and what could come of riding into them too often. Elizabeth, too, had been aware of the price, for when he'd turned from her in the schoolhouse, intent on going after Frome, she'd said, "Jess, don't do it his way!" And at the ranch she'd asked him to leave Grady Jones in the badlands.

But still there was a thing to be done, and the only difference now was in the manner in which he might do it. He looked at the flames climbing into the night, and he waited. After a while he heard the grind of a boot against sandy soil, and Grady Jones spoke from just beyond the rim of firelight. "All right, Jess. You've found me. Or I've found you. It all adds up to the same thing. Don't move. I've got a gun on you."

Loudon was crouched upon his haunches. He remained that way. He kept his hands showing plain. Jones came into the firelight. He was bearded and lean; his eyes glittered in the light. He looked from Loudon to where the gun belt lay upon the rock; he measured the distance and let the gun in his hand sag slightly.

Loudon said, "I fetched a shovel along, Grady. Now I don't want to use it. Throw your gun down. We'll ride to Helena, and I'll turn you over to the law."

Jones said, "What kind of a fool do you take me for?"

Loudon said, "It's not personal with me, Grady. Not any more. But you've got to pay for Clem one way or another."

"It's personal with me," Jones said. "I've hated you ever since I first saw that Frome had his eye on you as the man for promotion. It was personal that night we caught up with your friend, McSween. You said you never wanted to know which one of us put the noose around his neck and belted his horse out from under him. I'm the one took on that job."

For an instant the old anger ran strong in Loudon, but he kept his voice calm. "Then you're here to kill me, Grady?"

"That's the size of it," Jones said, and he raised his gun.

Loudon fell sidewards then, brushing away the

grubsack as he did so and bringing up his own gun. His first shot crashed out at the same time as Jones', and he kept shooting. Echoes beat wildly until it was as though an army had come again to the badlands. He felt dirt sting his face as a bullet pelted close to him, and he saw Jones, a black shapelessness beyond the fire, lurch forward and then stumble and fall. Loudon got up and reached for Jones and dragged him from the fire and turned him over and looked at him.

After that there was work for the shovel; and when he got the hole dug and Jones rolled into it, he thought of Joe McSween. He took Joe's five silver dollars out of his pocket and dropped them into the shallow grave and began heaving the dirt in. He went scouting the darkness then till he found Jones' horse back a piece. It was a Long Nine horse. He brought the horse up to the fire and hobbled it and rolled into his blanket and slept.

Came morning, and he rode west, heading out of the badlands, Jones' horse led behind him.

He slept near Castle Bend that night, and another morning found him upon prairie country. The sun was out again. After a while he drew rein and hipped around in his saddle and looked back toward the badlands, looked back to rock and desolation and the blank sky above it. He shook his head.

In late afternoon, he stepped down at Long Nine's corral. The yard was empty, and he supposed that most of the crew were on the trail to Miles. Smoke rose from the cook-shack and from the bunkhouse; a few of the boys were around. He untied the shovel from his saddle and took it to the blacksmith shop. He walked to the corral again and was unsaddling Jones' horse when Elizabeth came running from the house. She had on a printed calico today. She came to within arm's length, and she looked from him to Jones' horse and back again.

He said, "Know this: at the end I gave him his choice, but he wanted it to be guns between us. I've got my thinking straight now. I went into the badlands, but I've come out. I'll never go there again."

"Jess!" she cried. "Jess!"

"And I'm glad Frome broke free of me that day on the steamboat," he said. "Just the same, I hounded him into the river. Lately I've kept remembering that."

She said, "Charley Fuller is back. He heard about Frome, and he came back."

"That's good," he said.

"Frome was found, Jess. Right after you left. He's buried up there by Ollie. The lawyers were here again. His will has been read. He left everything to me."

He considered this. She stood patiently waiting. A cold breeze roamed the yard, and she shivered. At last he said, "I'll get what I have in the bunkhouse and be on my way."

She looked as though he had slapped her. "Why, Jess? Tell me why."

"Elizabeth," he said, "it's a million miles from the bunkhouse to the big house."

She bit at her lip and looked down, and then she said, "Jess, there was a time not long ago when I wondered if I could even aim a gun at a man, much less pull the trigger. But that day when Grady Jones walked into the barn at the Point, I knew that if either he or Frome climbed that ladder, I would aim the gun and pull the trigger. Does that tell you anything?" Suddenly she spread her hands, taking in all of Long Nine. "What good is this to me, Jess? I need you!"

She moved closer to him, and in her eyes he read the

fullness of her need. Not the need of boss for foreman, but the need that he himself had recognized the day he'd brought her from town to Long Nine the second time, the need to give some point to ambition, making it more than just cattle and land and being looked up to. No thing that he had sought would ever have been enough. The real fulfillment was to need and be needed in turn.

"I'll stay," he said.

A lock of her hair had fallen to stray across her cheek; he brushed it back into place. She smiled at him, but she shivered again from the touch of the breeze. He took off his coat and very gently placed it on her shoulders.